PRAISI

THIS WAS NEVER AL

"A modern-day youth basketball journey that brings the history of the game to life while blending the experiences of growing up. Basketball is the sport that extends beyond societal barriers and allows for interaction among the people, including Zeke, Lawrence, the coaches, Dr. Naismith, and even the Entity!"

HOWARD FISHER
Head Coach
Youth Men's Basketball Team for Team USA

"You needn't be a basketball expert to be captivated by *This Was Never About Basketball.* The novel is a charming and magical tale of enduring friendship, unlikely heroes, and finding the courage to do the right thing. This essential book has lessons and heroes that will stick with you for years to come. Leener has created a classic, a slam-dunk!"

ETHAN KLEIN
h3h3productions

"Created from a magical recipe that includes one part Sci-Fi, two parts basketball, and three parts friendship and adventure, *This Was Never About Basketball* adds up to a delightful page-turner that's all heart. Mr. Leener writes with a love for basketball equaled only by his love for spinning a deliciously good yarn. You will fall in love with the characters you'll meet, and you'll love even more the crazy places they'll take you!"

BOB DICKSON
Associate Professor of Communication &
Communication Department Chair
The Master's University

"A fun story with a few twists. It touches on family, friendship, the great game of basketball, and a bit of the supernatural. A wild ride and read!"

BOB DAVIS
Hall of Fame Radio Broadcaster
University of Kansas Basketball

"I was impressed with the character development of *This Was Never About Basketball.* Many of the characters reminded me of players I have coached over the years. The book captures the emotions of the young basketball player in all of us and is an insightful look at the journey many players find themselves on as they grapple towards their future. The book is thought-provoking and inspiring—a treat for the true basketball fan."

GREG HERRICK
Head Women's Basketball Coach
College of the Canyons

"I read the book, *This Was Never About Basketball*, because it was recommended by a friend who thought I might enjoy it. Knowing it was intended for an audience of teens and even pre-teens, I took a look, partially out of curiosity. I was pleasantly surprised. It was an interesting read, with a lot of humor and surprises. It was, in a way, a mystery novel with an interesting, twisting plot. Perhaps more importantly, it was well written and kept the attention of this 85-year-old. I recommend it to pre-teens, teens, and their dads, as well."

CHUCK YOUNG
Chancellor Emeritus
UCLA

"An exhilarating tale of adventure, excitement, friendship, and redemption, set against the backdrop of the game we all love. Leener does a magnificent job telling a modern coming-of-age story chock full of the types of real-world issues and circumstances facing today's youth. Joining Zeke and his crew on this thrilling adventure will deepen any young person's love and understanding of the game of basketball, while also providing more seasoned readers with a renewed appreciation for the sport and the role it played in their childhood."

JESSE MUÑOZ
Director of Public Relations & Sports Information
College of the Canyons

"Our actions, or in other words, our choices, have consequences, both good and bad. I love how Leener shows the struggle between both. He uses the lessons learned in the game of basketball and applies them to the game of life—teamwork, problem solving, and leadership."

GARETT TUJAGUE
Offensive Line Coach
University of Virginia Football

"The book brings a unique approach to the dilemmas that scholastic athletes often face. Zeke Archer in his own way finds that solution while entertaining the reader."

GUS ALFIERI
Author of *Lapchick: The Life of a Legendary Player and Coach in the Glory Days of Basketball* and *The Heart of a Champion*

"Leener's novel is unexpectedly powerful, perhaps because you wouldn't expect a story about sport-stealing aliens to carry such emotional weight. But, as its title suggests, *This Was Never About Basketball* is focused primarily on the journey and growth of its protagonist, Zeke, and uses this zany plot to help him reach his destination. This is a potent, positively charged novel that has a great message for young adults about the importance of leading by example and owning up to your own shortcomings."

RED CITY REVIEW

"Tee it up and let the big dog eat! If you like sports and the human experience, you will love this book!"

CHUCK LYON
Athletic Director & Dean of Physical Education, Kinesiology and Athletics, College of the Canyons

"The book was amazing in every single way. There was so much detail in every page that I couldn't put it down. I love how the author built up the suspense to the point where I had to start biting my nails. This is definitely a book every kid should read because they could learn a few life lessons. This book is definitely the best book I've ever read, and I'd definitely like to see a sequel for the book or even just another book from this author."

HAILEY STAR DOWTHWAITE
Avid reader and youth basketball player
Los Angeles

"*This Was Never About Basketball* is fabulous! I couldn't put it down and have never finished a book so quickly. My husband started it yesterday, and I'm sure he will love it as well. I look forward to seeing it in the movies."

ANNETTE FEIN
the author's mother-in-law

THIS WAS NEVER ABOUT BASKETBALL

CRAIG LEENER

Published by Green Buffalo Press.

For information, address Green Buffalo Press: www.greenbuffalopress.com.

Cover design by Tabitha Lahr
Interior text design by *BackStory Design*

A catalog record is available from the Library of Congress.
ISBN: 978-0-9905489-2-8 (print)
ISBN: 978-0-9905489-3-5 (e-book)

10 9 8 7 6 5 4 3 2 1

To Zak and Erika
for their love and encouragement

And to Andrea
for always being in my corner

CONTENTS

1

Better Step on It

I pushed open the cafeteria doors so hard, they swung back into me and knocked me on my butt.

Great way to start a story, right? But that's exactly how it happened.

Most kids in the cafeteria at Ernest T. McDerney Continuation School didn't notice my less than dignified entrance. The few who witnessed it snickered and went back to their lunches.

Continuation school in California is where they put high school kids who, mostly for disciplinary reasons, are at risk of not graduating. It's like an extended timeout that lasts the rest of your high school days. Not as bad as a life sentence, but some days it felt that way.

I picked myself up off the cafeteria's dusty linoleum floor as the unwelcome marriage of greasy pizza and pungent body spray greeted my nostrils. My destination was the table saved by Curtis Short and Roland "Stretch" Puckett, my best friends in the world.

Curtis, Stretch, and I used to attend Southland Central High School in Los Angeles. We were seniors and on the basketball team there until we were expelled exactly one month before this story begins. The reason why we were banished involved the game of basketball, and it changed the course of my life.

Basketball is my world. I have a basketball with me everywhere I go. Everything important in my life is connected to the sport. It's how I learn about the decisions people make and their motivations behind those decisions. If you want to know how a complete stranger would react under pressure, put a basketball in his hands and tell him to run a fast break with the game on the line. Does he pass to a teammate or pull up and shoot? Take it to the rim or bounce the ball off his foot and out of bounds? It's the ultimate study of the human condition.

Our team at Southland Central had advanced to the city finals before losing to Mid-City Prep. I could deal with losing. Heck, I'd lost a ton of basketball games in my seventeen years. But it was how we lost that has haunted me ever since. My temper got the better of me and I made an awful decision, right there on the basketball court, a place I hold sacred. Just one punch led to a brawl that led to my losing everything I'd worked for my entire life, including a college basketball scholarship to the University of Kansas.

That was February 26, our final day at Southland Central. Curtis and Stretch and I were sentenced to McDerney for the rest of our senior year. That's when all the weird things started happening.

"Ezekiel Archer, is there anywhere on earth you go without that stupid basketball?"

That was Rebecca Tuesday. She wasn't weird, and she was the only person except for my mother and Vice Principal Littwack who called me by my given first name, almost as if she already knew me. The reason why Rebecca had been discarded into McDerney was shrouded in mystery, at least as far as the school's general population was concerned, but I had overheard her tell one of her girlfriends that she had punched out a football player at her former high school. That meant she and I secretly had something in common.

"Don't listen to her, Zeke," Curtis said.

Curtis worshipped surfing the way I cherished basketball. He spent more time in the ocean than out of it. He also had the best jump shot I ever saw. Curtis once told me he'd take a bullet for me, with the qualifier that it had to come from the barrel of a small-caliber handgun and glance off his butt cheek.

"Yeah, can it, Rebecca," said Stretch, coming to my defense.

Stretch had acquired his nickname because he had surpassed six feet in the seventh grade and had grown steadily ever since, to reach six foot ten by our last year in high school, ensuring that his career choice as an undercover investigator would pose a challenge. Stretch was less enthusiastic about laying his life on the line for me than Curtis was, but I knew I could always count on him.

I set down my basketball on the seat of our table's empty fourth chair, so no one unfamiliar would think about eating lunch with the three of us. It hadn't always been that way, but I'd lost confidence in myself after I'd been expelled.

"Whaddaya got?" Stretch craned his neck as I opened my backpack.

"Kidding, right?" said Rebecca, eavesdropping from a nearby table, where she was gabbing with a bunch of girls. "You guys eat the same thing every day."

"Ignore her, dude, she doesn't know anything," Curtis said.

He was wrong there. Rebecca knew plenty. She was a straight-A student, and she was on top of all the important stuff happening at McDerney. She also did nice things for people, especially those she didn't know. She was tough and cute in a non-basketball way, but we didn't have a lot of time for girls.

Rebecca was right about our meal choices. Mom always packed American cheese on egg bread, plus carrots cut into squared-off spears for me. Curtis liked cream cheese and sliced pickles on white bread, no crust. Stretch favored PB&J.

The sound of activity erupting from a far corner of the cafeteria caught our attention. It came from Lawrence's table. This was a regular occurrence at lunch.

Lawrence was autistic and almost never spoke. He had his own table in the cafeteria because no one wanted to sit with him. My older brother, Wade, taught me to look after people who need help, so I'd taken Lawrence under my wing when I first met him, because it was the right thing to do. I'd even walked him home one day just the week before when some kids were bullying him after school. It reminded me of how Wade used to have my back whenever older kids picked on me.

Lawrence was a fourteen-year-old junior, so I figured he must have skipped a few grades prior to McDerney. I was intrigued by his interesting habits and his style, like wearing a pocket protector with seven freshly sharpened and beveled No. 2 pencils in it, for example. He also arrived daily at the cafeteria carrying a metal travel case containing a bowl and a spoon, a thermos of hot water, and the kind of foil-wrapped food brick you'd put into your backpack prior to boarding the Space Shuttle. This made Lawrence a target for thugs and bullies, meaning nearly the whole student body, especially McDerney's very own cement-head, Brock Decker. Brock was the sum total of the worst parts of all the campus felons you never wanted to meet, bound together by arrogance, faulty judgment, and an expensive haircut.

Brock was shouting at Lawrence now. I sprang to my feet, but Curtis blocked my path. "Bro, I've seen that look on your face before," Curtis said, referring to the very moment before I punched out someone at the city finals. I moved Curtis aside and arrived at Lawrence's table just as Brock was preparing to separate Lawrence from his lunch. His lips trembled, but he never looked up.

"Leave the kid alone," I said.

"Yeah, Brock, stop it right now." Rebecca was close behind me.

"Gee, Zeke. Now you need a girl to fight your battles for you," Brock said.

Brock knew firsthand that I didn't need anyone's help in the battle-fighting department because he was playing for Mid-City Prep in the finals when I was bounced from Southland Central.

"I'm tired of the stupid nerd bringing in that sad excuse for food," Brock said. "If he does it again, I'm gonna beat him over the head with it."

A nerd? No question about it. But stupid, Lawrence wasn't. I knew because he was in our first-period math class, where we witnessed his mystical relationship with numbers all the time.

I took a step toward Brock.

"Hold it right there, E-ze-ki-el." Vice Principal Littwack opted for the four-syllable version of my name. "You're supposed to have a reputation around here as a leader. Is this how you're choosing to lead?"

I was captain of my team at Southland Central, but I wasn't aware that anything positive I did there had followed me all the way to McDerney.

"And you, Mr. Decker. I thought you'd know better by now. Stand down, private."

Brock mumbled choice obscenities under his breath and headed back to his table to receive high fives from his knuckleheaded henchmen.

"Lawrence, you okay?" I asked.

No response and no eye contact either.

I thought it might help if I dispensed some big-brother-type advice. "Maybe if you brought a normal lunch to school like everyone else, jerks like Decker might leave you alone."

Still nothing. I shrugged it off and turned back toward my

table. Brock shot me a tough-guy look as I walked past him, but I shrugged that off too.

"C'mon, let's go shoot around," I said to the guys back at the table.

As we headed to the rear exit, Lawrence handed me a folded-up piece of paper. I opened it. His handwriting was measured and precise, the letters carefully formed and slanted to the right. I read the note to myself:

> *Better hurry.*

"What is it?" I asked.

Lawrence pulled a pencil from the seven in his pocket protector and wrote me another note. He tore it from his pad of paper, folded it in half, and held it out:

> *Freeze-dried chili mac 'n' beef. Dehydration process, preserves perishable food, makes it convenient for transport.*

"No, not that. You said something about hurrying up."

Lawrence repeated the process, and things went from weird to weirder:

> *Better step on it. They're planning to take the game away.*

"Who is? What game?" I now had a clearer understanding of why people thought Lawrence was odd.

"Basketball," Lawrence said. Yes, he actually said the word before writing me yet another note:

> *The 7th Dimension, an interdimensional energy being. Says it was the force behind the creation of basketball on Earth. Says it has decided to take the game away, and it's your fault. If you're planning to shoot around with your friends, you'd better step on it.*

2

Maybe We'll Get It Right This Time

I spent the rest of the school day speculating about what Lawrence's cryptic messages meant. Like I said, weird stuff started happening around that time at McDerney.

The school bell rang to signal the end of sixth period, and I couldn't wait to get out of there. Ever since I had been shown the door at Southland Central, school had felt like something I had to just survive.

The guys and I got on our bikes and rode down Bird Parkway to the rec center, where we always went after school to play pickup basketball until it got dark and was time to go home.

"Dude, I've got homework to do first," Curtis said as we locked our bikes at the entrance.

"That's a fine idea, Mr. Short."

That was rec center director, Vernon Shields, a real homework-first kind of guy. He had been the director for twenty-five years and always made sure it was a safe place for kids. Mr. Shields knew a whole bunch about arts and crafts, counseling, and nutrition—important stuff the person in charge needed to deal with. Beyond that, there wasn't a question about basketball he couldn't answer. We had heard stories about when Mr. Shields was head coach at nearby Jefferson Community College years earlier and led his team to a state championship.

Mr. Shields went to his office as Curtis set down his backpack in the library and pulled out his biology textbook. Stretch went to the kitchen to scrounge for food. Since he was nearly a foot taller than me, I gave him a pass for being hungry all the time.

I sat on the floor of the rec center's welcome room with my back against the wall and spun my basketball on my right index finger. That was how I coped with stress, by balancing my world, which was quite literally basketball, right there in front of me. My brother, Wade, taught me how to spin a basketball when I was just a kid. When Wade enlisted in the Marine Corps five years ago, I remember watching that ball go around and around until my finger bled.

"If you spin that thing any faster, it's going to take flight," Mr. Shields said. He could always tell when I had a lot on my mind. My world had spun off its axis when I got expelled, and I was unsuccessful in getting it back on track.

"Follow me," Mr. Shields said. "I've got something you might want to see."

When we reached his office door, Mr. Shields cleared space on the bulletin board outside and stuck two pieces of paper up there with thumbtacks. "These arrived in the mail a couple of weeks ago, but I've been busy and didn't open the envelope until this morning. Maybe it will cheer you up."

I read the top of page one:

3-on-3 Basketball Tournament

My stomach churned. I had the feeling my life was about to change course again.

"Do you think you could put a team together before the registration deadline?" Mr. Shields said with a smile.

Curtis and Stretch caught wind of our conversation and joined us at the bulletin board.

"I think so," was all I could think to say to Mr. Shields as I scanned the rest of the first page. It explained that Jefferson Community College was sponsoring a three-on-three basketball tournament open to local high school seniors. That was great. But then the bad news kicked in. The registration deadline was twenty-four hours away, the team entry fee was one hundred dollars, which we had almost no chance of raising, and the tournament was on Saturday. This coming Saturday.

The top team would move on to compete for the western regional championship a couple of weeks away, in mid-April, at the birthplace of basketball, the University of Kansas.

Wait a second. The University of Kansas? The college that had offered me a basketball scholarship and then taken it away after the incident at the city finals? The universe was playing a cruel joke on me.

Page two of the flyer contained the tournament's rules, thirteen in all, covering everything from player eligibility to free-throw shooting distance to sportsmanship.

Rule number five, in particular, was specific and left nothing to chance:

> *Good sportsmanship is expected of all players. The team captain shall control himself and his teammates at all times. If anyone on a team shows evident intent to injure a player on the other team, the offending team shall be disqualified from the tournament.*

That last part had a familiar ring to it. I was no stranger to the consequences of violating rule number five, and I'd paid a heavy toll for disregarding it at Southland Central.

Now, out of nowhere, we had the chance for a different outcome. I turned to face Curtis and Stretch and struggled to find the right words. "You guys in? Maybe we'll get it right this time."

Curtis looked me squarely in the eye. "Why not, dude?"

Stretch reached down and jabbed me in the chest a couple of times with his boney finger. "I'm in," he said. "Let's go get us some hardware."

And some money for the entry fee, I thought.

3

Hey, They Were There a Minute Ago

There was still daylight left, so we went out the back door of the center to the basketball court. Our second home. For an outdoor court, it was a good one, and Mr. Shields saw to it that it stayed that way.

The court had smooth concrete, freshly painted lines, and regulation-size backboards with bright-orange rims. The rims were draped with steel-chain nets, which last longer outdoors than their nylon counterpart. The high-pitched metal-clank noise they make when a long jump shot glides through is a sweet sound unlike any other.

But not this day. The rims and nets were gone.

I turned to go get Mr. Shields, but he was already standing in the doorway, mouth wide open and face frozen somewhere between confusion and irritation. "What in the world . . . ?" Mr. Shields said. I had a feeling he wanted to say something more colorful, but he chose his words carefully, because that's what adults in charge are supposed to do. "They were here an hour ago. How could they just disappear?"

Good question. It was the second time in a matter of hours that something bizarre had happened related to basketball. The first was when Lawrence scribbled gibberish in the cafeteria about something called the 7th Dimension.

Mr. Shields left us standing there and went back inside the rec center.

"Not good—we've got work to do to get ready for the tournament," I told the guys. We left it up to Mr. Shields to figure out what had happened and went our separate ways into the night.

I rode my bike to my apartment and waited for my mom to get home. Mom worked as a nurse across town at Mikan Memorial Hospital. She usually got home in time to make dinner unless she was working overtime, like that night, in which case I wouldn't see her until the next morning, when she'd be packing my lunch.

The apartment was emptier since Wade had joined the marines and left for boot camp. After that, my parents argued a whole bunch until my father moved to Colorado. I hadn't seen him since.

After the divorce, my dad mailed me a letter to explain why he had left. I read it and then squirreled it away somewhere. I don't recall much of what it said, because it was so long ago. But I remember him telling me about being in the army and serving our country in the Iraq War and how the terrible things he witnessed there gave him nightmares and left him feeling disconnected from our family. My dad sent me more letters in the years that followed, but I never opened them.

Basketball always helps me stuff my problems down so deep that I don't have to feel them gnawing at my insides, so I spun my ball as I settled in front of the TV to zone out with a college game.

I must have fallen asleep, because "Honey, wake up!" were the next words I heard. It was morning and my mom was still in her nurse's uniform. "You need to get ready for school, son."

I rubbed the sleep from my eyes. "Mom, there's something I need to talk to you about."

I told her about the three-on-three tournament, how Mr. Shields thought it would be a good experience for Curtis and Stretch and me, and how uneasy I felt about getting back into organized ball. "We've got to sign up for it today by five o'clock." My mouth felt dry and there was an empty feeling in the pit of my stomach. "We need to come up with a hundred bucks for our entry fee."

Curtis was good with money, when he actually had some. Stretch, not so much.

After what happened at Southland Central, I wanted to quit school for good and get a job so I could pay my own way, but my mom said to forget it. My job, she told me, was going back to school and earning good grades so I could get a college education. The funny thing was, I had that lined up at the University of Kansas—until I blew it. Now it felt like I was starting from scratch, and I was supposed to be graduating from McDerney at the beginning of June.

"The guys and I don't have that kind of money, and I don't want to ask anyone for it, including you."

Mom leaned over and gave me a hug. When she let go, tears welled up in her eyes. "I worry about Wade," she said as she took a deep breath. "He was always the headstrong one." Wade was a staff sergeant in the Marine Corps Forces Special Operations Command in Afghanistan. He was living in a war zone eight thousand miles from home. "But with you, I've always felt you'd figure it out in your own time."

Figuring out my life seemed like a long way off. I watched as my mom reached high up in the pantry and brought down an old coffee can. I knew it was there even though I never saw her put anything in or take anything out. That was about to change. She stuck her hand inside and pulled out five folded-up twenty-dollar bills.

"Here, take this." As I took hold, Mom gripped onto the cash for a moment. When she finally let go, she howled in laughter as tears escaped onto her light-blue hospital scrubs. "I'll put it on your tab."

"Pay you back. Promise." My mom never let me down. I had a running tab I'd never be able to repay.

I took a quick shower and went to my bedroom to pack my stuff and pocket the hundred bucks. I looked down at the usual spot on the floor where I kept my basketball, but it wasn't there. I checked the closet. Not there, either.

"Mom, have you seen my ball?"

"No."

"I had it last night when I was watching the game."

"The answer is still no."

This was the *third* strange basketball-related thing to happen in the space of one day. I searched every inch of the apartment. My ball was gone. I could feel the hairs on the back of my neck standing at attention.

I couldn't be late for school because that would mean having to deal with Vice Principal Littwack. Fewer prospects in my world were worse than that.

4

The Nerd Is Nuts

I snapped my bike lock onto the steel rack in front of the school just as the bell rang. Good grief, eight o'clock. I sprinted to my first-period math class and turned the door handle. It was locked. I knocked on the door. No response. I looked up at the clock in the hallway outside the classroom.

"That's right, Ezekiel, it's eight oh five." It was the stone-cold voice of Vice Principal Littwack. "Do you know what a 'tardy lockout' is?"

"No, sir."

"When the bell rings, we lock all the classroom doors and any student still out here wandering the hallways is rewarded with two hours of detention."

"Two hours?"

"This afternoon, two thirty in study hall. Bring your homework. And it's not a scrimmage, Mr. Archer. Leave your basketball in your locker."

This was not happening to me. "I can't today, sir. I have something really important I have to do after school." I needed to get to Jefferson Community College by five o'clock to turn in our tournament application with our hundred-dollar entry fee.

"The only place you have to be after school, young man, is study hall," Mr. Littwack said. "I can arrange to make it three hours, if you'd prefer."

"No, sir, that won't be necessary."

Mr. Littwack loosened the knot of his tie and said something I didn't expect to hear from him.

"People look up to you, Ezekiel. Believe it or not, even Mr. Decker does. It's important for you to lead by example here at McDerney. Take responsibility, son."

Mr. Littwack was pointing out a side of me I didn't know existed. I knew a lesson was buried in there somewhere, but I didn't have time to figure it out. I needed to concentrate on how I was going to get from study hall to Jefferson on my bike in less than thirty minutes.

Mr. Littwack unhooked a key ring from his belt and fumbled through the tangled mass of metal until he found the key he needed.

"Nice of you to join us," said Mr. Appleton as I walked into the classroom and found my seat alongside Curtis and Stretch.

"Sorry I'm late, sir."

Mr. Appleton was in mid-lesson at the chalkboard, writing out a massive formula. The room was a sea of glazed-over eyes, except for Lawrence, who stared at the board without blinking.

"Dude, where's your ball?" Curtis whispered.

"Good question," I shot back. "I looked everywhere. Really weird. But I've got a bigger problem."

At the time, I didn't know the half of it.

Lawrence raised his hand. The room fell silent in anticipation.

"Yes, what is it, Lawrence?" Mr. Appleton said.

Lawrence rarely spoke. When he did, it was always an adventure, because he used few words and they were blunt. I liked that about him.

"It doesn't work."

The three girls sitting in the front row giggled.

"What doesn't?" Mr. Appleton said.

"Your formula. It's flawed."

"Perhaps you'd like to—"

Lawrence didn't wait for Mr. Appleton to finish that sentence. Before the teacher knew what hit him, Lawrence was up there erasing numbers and letters with his sleeve and replacing them with other numbers and letters. Then he went back to his seat.

"Lawrence, I don't think . . ." Lawrence raised his hand again. "Yes, Lawrence," Mr. Appleton said, a look of irritation rolling across his face as he adjusted his glasses.

"It works. Check it."

Mr. Appleton stared at the formula. His lips moved, but no words came out. Then he turned around, a hard smile on his face as he waved the white flag. "So it does. Thank you, Lawrence."

The three girls in the front row giggled again. I had the urge to walk over to Lawrence and give him a fist bump, but I was already in enough trouble for being late to class. The victory would have to be a silent one. When math ended, I had a few minutes before our next class to fill in the guys on how my afternoon was shaping up.

"Detention? Good luck with that, dude," Curtis said.

"I'm stuck there till four thirty, then I've got to get to Jefferson by five to sign us up, and that place is not exactly around the corner. I'm worried I won't make it in time."

"Dude, I'm worried about why you're standing here without your ball," Curtis said. "Where is it?"

"Wish I knew," I said. "It's totally freaking me out."

"Maybe you were sleepwalking last night and flushed it down the toilet," Stretch said.

"You're not helping, bro," Curtis said.

Lawrence must have heard the last part of our conversation about my ball. "It's starting," he said, as he balanced an overloaded backpack in one hand and his aluminum lunch crate in the other.

"He's right, we'd better get to our next class," Stretch said. "I don't want to get taken down by Littwack. I'm not cut out for detention."

Lawrence raised his voice as if to indicate that we hadn't heard him right the first time. "*It's starting!* The 7th Dimension is taking the game away."

Here we go again, I thought. More gibberish. I felt like telling Lawrence he wasn't making any sense, but I didn't want to hurt his feelings. "We're kind of busy right now," I whispered. "Let us get back to you on this taking-the-game-away thing."

Lawrence's face reddened. He glanced around in every direction but mine before setting down his things and scribbling out another note:

> *Nets and rims at the rec center, step one. Your missing basketball, step two. Don't you get it? IT'S STARTING.*

That sealed it. This kid was nuts. "And you know this how?" I said.

Lawrence didn't answer. He simply pointed to his pocket protector, the one with the seven No. 2 pencils, graphite tips pointing skyward like a row of tiny missiles ready for launch.

"So the pencils are telling you." I almost pulled a muscle trying to stifle a smile, but Lawrence didn't waver. He wrote me another note:

> *I use my pencils to intercept and decode their communiqués. The 7th Dimension brought the game here in 1891. It just decided to take it away forever. The voices are saying it's YOUR fault.*

5

Can You Make an Exception?

Sitting in detention, I had my chemistry textbook opened as a decoy as I stared off into the heavens and took stock of my life, which looked bleak. On the plus side, I was in detention, which gave me ample time to dwell on everything in my world that was going wrong.

On the minus side, I had blown a full-ride scholarship to a Midwestern basketball powerhouse. I was marooned at a school for social outcasts and misfits. Vandals had stolen the most important part of the rec center's basketball court. My mom had taken away my ball—or at least I thought she must have, because that was the only reasonable explanation for its disappearance, but it didn't matter because I didn't need it anymore since we could no longer play basketball at the center because the rims and nets were gone. . . .

Then toss in the geeky kid in my math class who blamed

me for a decision by space aliens to ship the game to another planet.

That was everything.

Thwap!

Not quite. I was all of seven minutes into detention, and Brock had hit me in the back of the neck with a spitball.

"That will be quite enough, Brock." That was Mrs. Vanderhorst, the school librarian. She wore her gray hair in a bun and a sweater buttoned up to her neck. Vice Principal Littwack had put Mrs. Vanderhorst in charge of the study hall because it was next door to the library. Detention duty was an added bonus for her.

If Brock looked up to me, as Mr. Littwack said he did, then he had a funny way of showing it. I wiped the spittle from the back of my neck and braced for another assault. That assault never arrived, because by the time the bell rang at four thirty, Brock had been fast asleep with his feet propped up on the chair in front of him for most of the previous two hours.

I picked up my backpack and raced out of there. When I got to my bike, I learned there was one more item to add to the minus column—a flat tire. I weighed my options. There was only one.

Run. *Fast.*

I raced down Chamberlain Drive and didn't stop until I reached Jefferson Community College at the corner of West Way and Baylor Boulevard. I stopped to catch my breath. It was the first time I had been on campus at Jefferson since the high school championship game.

I found the information desk and asked the attendant

where signups were for the three-on-three tournament. He pointed toward the gym.

"Coach Kincaid, that-a-way."

"Can you tell me what time it is, please?"

"Five o'clock."

I took off for the gym. Along the way, I wondered how I would break the news to Curtis and Stretch that I had missed the application deadline. When I arrived at the gym, I realized that I had no idea where Coach Kincaid's office was.

"Hey, dweeb." Great, it was Brock. He smirked and shot a dismissive glance toward an office door. "Over there."

How in the world did Brock get to Jefferson before I did?

"Later, dweeb," Brock said as he bounced away, tossing a set of car keys up and down with one hand for emphasis.

Coach Kincaid was sitting at his desk wearing standard coach-type gear—gym shorts and a polo shirt with the school mascot emblazoned on it. The mascot was a lion, a symbol of wisdom and courage. I was in need of both.

I sized up the room. There were trophies everywhere. The walls were covered with team photos and plaques.

Coach Kincaid had been in the stands for the city-title game at Jefferson the month before when life as I knew it ended. I had never met him before. He looked up as I came in.

"Hello, Zeke."

"Hi, Coach, my name is Ezekiel Archer. . . ."

I was off to a shaky start. I glanced over Coach Kincaid's shoulder for a split second and saw a photo of him standing alongside Mr. Shields. They were celebrating and hoisting a trophy into the air. Coach Kincaid looked a lot younger in the photo and wore a Jefferson basketball uniform. Mr. Shields had what must have been the game ball tucked under his arm.

"I'm here to sign up for the three-on-three tournament, sir."

Coach Kincaid lowered his head and released a heavy sigh. There was a pained expression on his face. "I'm sorry, Zeke, but you missed the deadline." I don't exactly remember what happened next, but I think my life flashed before me. "It's five oh five. The deadline was five o'clock."

I thought about explaining to Coach Kincaid about detention and the flat tire and how much Curtis and Stretch and I needed to play in that tournament. Then I remembered something Wade had said years ago to the man working at the amusement park when I wanted to ride the big roller coaster but wasn't tall enough, according to park rules.

"Do you think you could make an exception?"

Coach Kincaid pressed his fist against his lips. I couldn't tell if he was thinking of a way to let me down easy or concealing a smile.

"An exception?" Coach Kincaid said, answering my question with a question.

"Yes, sir. An exception. Please."

Coach Kincaid motioned for me to hand him our entry form. He studied it and took a deep breath before rendering his decision. "When someone introduces an exception to a rule, it reinforces the fact that the rule in question is actually in force."

What?

"Yes, sir."

"I'll grant your request for an exception under two conditions."

"Sir?"

"Number one, that we see better sportsmanship in this gymnasium than we did at the city finals. And number two, that you call me 'Coach' instead of 'sir.'"

"Yes, sir—I mean, Coach. Thank you, sir—*Coach*."

I handed Coach Kincaid our entry fee, and in return he gave me back the copy of the tournament rules that had been attached to the application form.

"Good luck. We'll see you on Saturday."

"Thanks, Coach."

As I made my way along Baylor Boulevard on the long trek back, I felt a glimmer of something I hadn't experienced in a long time: Hope.

I had put so much of my heart and soul into basketball. The rewards were there along the way in the form of friendships and trophies and opportunities to take my game to a new level. But after that punch in the city finals, it felt like I had lost everything—until now.

I was being given another chance. I had no idea why. Competition would be fierce on Saturday. Our odds of winning would be long. Even if we were lucky enough to pull it off, I had no idea how we would get all the way to eastern Kansas for the western regional finals.

The stars were out by the time I made it back to McDerney. There were lots of bikes at the bike rack, but it wasn't hard to spot mine. It was the one with the front tire that was so flat, it looked as though the rubber at the bottom was glued to the pavement. I unlocked my bike and began the walk of shame home.

"Not going to get far on that thing."

It was Rebecca, appearing out of the darkness.

"What are you still doing here?" I said.

"I should be asking you the same thing," she replied.

I wanted to tell Rebecca about the tournament and how Coach Kincaid had gone the extra mile to get us in. I wanted to tell her how we had a chance to visit the place where basketball began and, for the first time in a long while, I had reason to get out of bed in the morning.

"Nothing," was all I said. "Just basketball."

"What is it with you guys and that dumb game?"

I barely knew this girl and she was giving me grief. I wasn't sure if I wanted to take her into my confidence or tell her to take a hike.

"I heard some kids talking about how you, like, went nuts at some big basketball game last month at Jefferson. Cops, blood, everything. They said that's how you ended up at McDerney."

"There wasn't much blood. It was nothing," I said, but that was a lie because it was the biggest something that had ever happened to me. In some weird way, I was beginning to feel close to Rebecca. I wanted to tell her the real story, but instead I said it was late and I needed to get home.

"Me, too. Where do you live? Maybe we could walk home together."

It turned out Rebecca lived a few blocks from my apartment.

On our way home, I told her everything.

"We were playing Brock Decker's team, Mid-City Prep, for the city championship. Brock and I grew up together and we used to be friends, but that changed a long time ago." I told Rebecca how we trailed Mid-City Prep by one point with a few seconds left to play when I ran a fast break that would have produced the winning basket. "I faked a pass to Curtis on my right before throwing a wraparound to Stretch, who was barreling down the lane on my left."

"You got expelled for throwing a behind-the-back pass?"

Rebecca knew a lot more about basketball than she let on. She had a sense of humor too. "I'm going to pretend you didn't say that," I said before continuing. "Stretch went up for a dunk that would have iced it, but before he could slam the ball down through the hoop, Brock clotheslined him."

"He what?"

I explained that Brock had hooked the big man in the throat with his outstretched arm. Stretch hit the floor hard and the ball flew out of bounds. Both referees missed it. They never called a foul.

"When I saw Brock do that on purpose to one of my best friends, all this anger exploded inside me. I guess I just snapped."

Rebecca's eyes widened as I told her how I confronted Brock and took a giant swing at him. Brock ducked, and the punch meant for him hit one of the referees squarely on the jaw. "The ref went down like a sack of potatoes. Curtis realized what happened and jumped into the mess and started swinging too."

When it was over, the referee I slugged went to the hospital in an ambulance. The referee I didn't slug declared Mid-City Prep the winner by forfeit, and the police escorted Brock and me and the guys out of the gym. The next day, all four of us were expelled. Three days after that, I got a letter in the mail from the Athletics Department at the University of Kansas.

"They revoked my scholarship, the very same KU that's hosting the western regional three-on-three tournament in a couple of weeks. So I might get the chance to go to the campus after all, but for a way shorter stay." I hadn't told anyone the full story of what happened until that moment. "So that's my deal. How did you end up at McDerney?"

"Can't tell you right now."

My heart sank. "I just poured my guts out to you and you can't tell me anything? No way."

"That's mine," Rebecca said, motioning to the brown house with the white picket fence we were standing in front of. "It's late. Maybe next time. Guess I'll see you tomorrow."

I had gotten so caught up in telling my story that I'd lost track of time. I wasn't ready to say goodbye to Rebecca, but it wasn't up to me. I pushed my bike the rest of the way home. When I got there, I was surprised to find Stretch standing in front of my apartment building.

"Man, I've been waiting here forever," he said. "Where have you been?"

Where do I start? I thought. "Nowhere. Just the junior college. I turned in the application for the tournament. We're good to go."

Stretch curled his shoulders forward and drooped his head. He was no longer the hulking, happy-go-lucky guy I knew.

"I can't play on Saturday," he said, shuffling his feet.

What?

"That's funny. I thought I heard you say you can't play on Saturday."

"Shut up. I have to help my dad paint the inside of a warehouse 'cause he can't afford to hire a crew. He's not giving me a choice."

We'd just gotten knocked out of the tournament—before it had even started.

6

It Must Be an Inside Job

I dragged my bike up the stairs, banging the rear tire off every step leading to apartment number 7. I heard a door creak open across the hall.

"Cheese 'n' crackers, Zeke. What's all the racket?"

That was our neighbor, Mrs. Fenner. She was about an eight out of ten on the snoopiness scale. Mrs. Fenner claimed to be hard of hearing, except for the times when I dropped a pin in the hallway.

"It's nothing, Mrs. Fenner. Just me. And my bike. Flat tire. Need to fix it."

I went inside my apartment and found a note from my mom:

Working late.
Dinner in fridge.
Love you.

It was a long day, but I wasn't hungry at all. I found Wade's toolbox in the hall closet and pulled out his tire repair kit. Wade used to fix my flat tires all the time. Before he shipped off to San Diego for boot camp, he showed me how to fix them myself.

It wasn't hard to locate the problem—a rusty nail had impaled the front tire. I thought about how my life was like the tire with that rusty nail in it, rolling along fine until the unexpected came along, and then everything stopped.

I pulled out the nail with a pair of pliers, patched the tube, and pumped the tire back up, just the way Wade had taught me. If only it were that easy to fix the broken parts of my life, I thought. I looked around the apartment again for my errant basketball. Still MIA.

I unlaced my high-tops and settled in for the night. I thought about how much I needed to speak with my brother. I used to write Wade letters all the time when he first joined the corps, but it was a long time since the last one.

Wade was up to his neck in real-life trouble in Afghanistan, so I figured the last thing he needed to hear was how my life had fallen apart because of my own stupid decision.

Then I remembered Wade telling me before he deployed that the Marine Corps was good at getting mail to marines overseas, so I should write him if I needed to. I tore a blank sheet of paper from my notebook, took a seat at the kitchen table, and filled in my brother on everything that had gone wrong.

I wasn't in the habit of letting Wade down, so those were the toughest words I had ever written to him. I brought him up to date on what a mess my life had become, and then I started writing about Rebecca. I couldn't believe I was telling Wade about a girl I was interested in. That was a new development for the Archer brothers.

On the bright side, there's a girl at school named Rebecca who I think is cool, although she's kind of tough and I'm not exactly sure why she's at McDerney. Right now she won't tell me, but I'm reasonably certain it's because she punched some football jock in the face. Mom is doing okay, but I wish she wouldn't work so much. Don't worry, she always remembers to pay the monthly storage bill for your pickup truck. I haven't heard from Dad in a long time. Last thing is, there's this nerdy autistic kid at school named Lawrence. He's a fourteen-year-old junior, which is kinda strange because the minimum age at McDerney is supposed to be sixteen, so I'm guessing he skipped a couple of grades because he's really smart, especially in math class, but it's a mystery as to why he's there. I look after him at school because no one else does. I wonder if that reminds you of anyone. Anyway, Lawrence keeps telling me something about basketball moving to a distant galaxy. I wonder if they'll let me play for the team there, because I'm having a heck of a time finding a game here on Earth. I don't know when I'll see you next, but I hope it's soon. Stay safe.

Zeke

I took an envelope out of my desk and addressed it to Wade with the special codes the military uses to get mail to soldiers overseas.

The next morning, Thursday, I left earlier than usual so I could mail Wade's letter on the way to school. I was riding down Drexler Drive toward the post office when I saw a bunch of police cars parked in front of Chip's Sporting Goods.

Chip's was my go-to sporting goods store. The owner, Chip Spears, was a good guy who knew a lot about basketball. When I rode up to the front of the store, I saw Chip talking with a policeman.

"Thank you, Officer Bryant," Chip was saying as the officer closed his notebook and headed back to his squad car.

"Hey, Chip. What's going on?"

"It's the darnedest thing, Zeke. I came in to open the store and realized we'd been burglarized. I went in and looked around, and the only stuff missing was the basketball gear." Chip rubbed his forehead, a look of disbelief on his face. "Basketballs, backboards, uniforms—the works. Officer Bryant thinks it might be an inside job, because there's no evidence of a break-in and the alarm never went off."

That was weird. Chip said something about not being sure how he would be able to afford to replace everything, but his voice trailed off as he walked away.

I needed a new ball. Now I'd have to buy it from a different store.

I mailed the letter to Wade and rode the rest of the way to McDerney. I remembered Lawrence's crazy notes about the end of basketball as we knew it. I couldn't wait to tell him about the break-in at Chip's. Then I had a crazy thought.

Maybe there was a connection.

7

What About the Pencils?

I met up with the guys in the cafeteria at noon. There wasn't a lot of conversation. Not much to say, really, with no tournament on Saturday and little hope of a basketball game breaking out anytime soon.

It wasn't important to talk about what we all had for lunch, because it never changed. What was different at our table, however, was the fourth chair. It was empty. I usually put my basketball there, but since my ball had been abducted by aliens or whatnot, the fourth chair was no longer my friend. We were fair game, and for reasons unknown, Rebecca got up from her usual table with her girlfriends and walked over.

"Anyone sitting here?"

"Suit yourself," Stretch said.

"Why the long face, Mr. Horse?" I couldn't believe Rebecca had said that. Stretch was a lanky guy with an unusually long face, so it was hardly a compliment. He was already down in the dumps, feeling responsible for our withdrawal from the three-on-three tournament, so if his face seemed longer than usual, it was for good reason.

"Shut up, Rebecca," was all Stretch could muster on short notice.

"Don't mind him," I said. "He's having a bad day. Grab a seat."

We had never had anyone sit with us at McDerney before—especially not a girl. Rebecca parked her tray next to my lunch bag, pulled her long brown hair into a ponytail, and dug in.

I looked across the cafeteria and noticed Lawrence flying solo. For once, I envied him. No small talk, just food in a foil pouch, a thick math textbook, and a whole bunch of pencils.

"Dude, do you think you can get your hundred bucks back from Coach Kincaid?" Curtis said. Good question. It had taken everything I had to get us into the tournament. The thought of asking Coach Kincaid for another exception was too much to bear.

"Refund? Not a chance." Brock must have fallen out of the sky, because I didn't see him slither over. "The college already spent it on extra security once they heard you losers signed up for the tournament."

"Beat it, Brock."

Really, Rebecca?

"I see the loser table has a spokeswoman now," Brock said. "Maybe she'll take a swing at me too?" With that, Curtis shot up and stepped toward Brock before I could intercept him.

"Again, Mr. Decker?" Vice Principal Littwack had seen this play out before and wasn't going to let it get out of hand. "Don't you have someplace better to be?"

"I can think of somewhere," said Rebecca, clearly taking her spokeswoman role to heart.

How did Brock know we couldn't play on Saturday? None of us ever spoke to him.

"That freak Lawrence knows a lot about your basketball schedule," Brock said. "He might make a better press agent than Rebecca."

"That's enough, Brock, or your next stop will be detention," Mr. Littwack said.

Brock managed to get in the last word as he walked away. "Bummer, losers. I was looking forward to a rematch."

After that there was a lot of eating going on but not much talking, until Rebecca broke the silence.

"If I'm going to serve as group spokesperson, I'll need to know the details of everything affecting the group." Rebecca flashed a smile after she said that, so I knew not to take her too seriously, but she seemed sincere in her interest, so we filled her in.

"Stretch has to help his dad paint a warehouse on Saturday, so there's no big man in the post, and no team. It's that simple," Curtis told her. "I was asking Zeke if he thought he could get his money back from Coach Kincaid."

"How much?" Rebecca asked.

"One hundred dollars," I replied. "Borrowed it from my mom. Not sure what I'm going to say to her if I can't get it back."

Rebecca raised an eyebrow. "Either of you two boys ever pick up a paint brush?" That was aimed at Curtis and me.

"What's that supposed to mean?" Curtis said.

"I am one step ahead of you, Beks," Stretch said.

I loved Stretch like a brother, but the only person he was ever one step ahead of was the opposing center for Mid-City Prep. And "Beks"? What was that about?

"Why don't the three of you go over to the warehouse tomorrow night and paint it yourselves, like, as a team," Rebecca said.

You know how once in a while something is right in front of your face, so close that you can't see it? That's the best excuse I have for why I hadn't thought of it first.

"I'm not sure my dad will go for that," Stretch said.

"Sure he will, dude," Curtis said. "Besides, how hard could it be?"

"Yeah, what could go wrong?" I said, trying to sound as optimistic as Curtis.

I had a feeling we were going to find out exactly what could go wrong. We agreed to meet up at Stretch's house in the evening to speak with Mr. Puckett about our plan to help Stretch paint the warehouse the night before the tournament. Then we went our separate ways for fifth period.

I walked by Lawrence's table on my way out of the cafeteria.

"Yo, what have you got there?" I asked him.

Lawrence took a spoonful from a bowl of a foreign substance I could not identify. Then another. "Chili mac 'n' beef," he said, his mouth still full. "Want some?"

"Maybe next time." Lawrence's eyes danced around the cafeteria as I sat down at his table. "I heard there was a burglary last night over at Chip's Sporting Goods. Know anything about that?" Silence. "Cops and everything. I saw Chip this morning, and he filled me in. Just basketball gear, nothing else. The police think it might be an inside job." More silence. "Know anything about it?"

Lawrence continued to eat his lunch as if I weren't there. I looked at my watch. If this went on any longer, I would be late to my fifth-period journalism class. This kid was a tough nut to crack.

"Guess I'll see you later," I said. I was two steps from the door when I heard Lawrence's voice. I couldn't make out what he said, and that put me at a crossroads. Should I double back for a chance to crack the McDerney Rain Man code, or leave and make it to journalism class before the bell?

"Lawrence, I didn't hear what you said." I headed back to his table.

He scribbled something on a piece of paper and handed it to me:

> *I'm not supposed to talk about it anymore.*
> *They warned me.*

The bell rang for the start of fifth period. It seemed longer and louder than usual. A pang of regret wiggled across the lining of my stomach. I squeezed my eyes shut and opened them. Lawrence was still there. I was in too deep to stop.

"Who warned you?" Silence. "Who are you talking about?" Silence again.

Was Lawrence messing with me? I rolled the tension from my shoulders as I prepared to make another run at him. "I consider myself to be your friend. You can tell me. It'll stay between the two of us. You have my word."

I paused to think about what I had said. Friendship, I had learned, was a commitment made by two people to look after each other's well-being. I could tell that Lawrence had something important to say, but maybe the hesitation was his way of protecting me in return.

He scanned every corner of the cafeteria as he packed away his lunch tools. I had no idea what he was going to say, but I was hoping it wouldn't have anything to do with pencils.

"Promise?" he said.

"Promise."

Lawrence rocked from side to side out of what seemed to be nervousness. "It's the pencils."

Ever have one of those days? "What about the pencils?"

"It's how I hear them."

It was too late to bail out. I didn't know where this conversation would lead, but I sure as heck was going to see it through. "Who are 'they'?" He wrote it down:

> *All I know is, they live in the roots of trees.*

Things were getting weird again. Lawrence seemed to believe his own words, and that made me think he'd gone bonkers. I felt sorry for him, but a voice in my head told me to keep digging.

"What are they telling you?"

Just then, Mr. Littwack came through the cafeteria's main doors and headed right for us as Lawrence wrote out the rest:

> *They're saying they realize now that bringing basketball here was a mistake. They're taking it back, a little at a time.*

Ever notice that a straightjacket is never around when you need one? Lawrence didn't flinch when he delivered the knockout blow, and he didn't write it down—he said it: "Basketball will cease to exist on the third Friday in April."

"That's how long you two will be marooned in detention if you don't hightail it to fifth period this instant."

Most students at McDerney knew where they stood with Mr. Littwack. Now Lawrence did too.

As I hustled to class, I tried to make sense of everything Lawrence had communicated to me. I figured he was making it up, because it was too insane to be real. But with so many bizarre incidents happening around basketball lately, I had to leave open the possibility that what he was saying might be true.

If that were the case, there was trouble ahead, because I could not imagine the world, or my life, without basketball.

8

Are You Out of Your Mind?

I rode past Chip's Sporting Goods on my way home from school. The store was closed. I noticed a sign hanging in the window, so I rode up for a closer look. I read it and then slumped down on my bike seat:

Store closed indefinitely
due to burglary investigation.
If you need sports equipment,
try Global Mega-Sports on Havlicek Expressway.

Global Mega-Sports was hands down the largest sporting goods store in Los Angeles. It carried everything anyone could ever want, but we always bought our gear at Chip's. When Chip heard that Wade had enlisted in the marines, he stopped by the rec center to deliver a new basketball, telling me that

Wade would make it home safely before I could wear out the ball. I doubt Chip ever dreamed I would lose the ball first, or even that his store would suffer the loss of its entire basketball inventory because of what appeared to be an inside job.

Add to the mix the rims and nets disappearing from the center, then throw in Lawrence's gloom-and-doom hypothesis, and there was only one conclusion left to draw: basketball was slipping away. My best chance to hang onto the sport I loved was Saturday's three-on-three tournament. To get there, all roads led to Mr. Puckett.

Curtis and I met up in front of Stretch's house on Walton Way at 8:00 p.m. We needed to convince Mr. Puckett that we were capable of painting an entire warehouse in the middle of the night all by ourselves, despite two of us having no painting experience whatsoever.

Stretch had a theory that his father would be in a more agreeable mood after he had dinner, ideally a meal that included beer and a sizeable second helping. We were about to test Stretch's theory.

"You what?" said Mr. Puckett after we explained our plan and the reason behind it. His face reddened. "You boys have got a lot of moxie."

Mr. Puckett took the last swig from his can of beer and looked at his son, who I could see was clearly fighting back tears. "You lads must really want to play in this tournament," Mr. Puckett said. "I'd like to help you out, but business has been slow for a while now, and I need this job to run smoothly."

Mr. Puckett explained that he would already be working

all day Friday, so there was no way he would have the stamina to keep painting through the night. "I can't be there, and I can't take the chance on you boys. I'm really sorry."

We apologized to Mr. Puckett for coming up with a plan that was not fully baked. Then Curtis and I left to go home.

"Nice try, dude," said Curtis as we stood on Stretch's front lawn. "Guess I'll see you at school tomorrow."

I rode to my apartment and went to bed before my mom got home from the hospital. I knew I would eventually have to face her, but I avoided her the next morning by leaving for school before she woke up.

The ride to McDerney seemed longer than usual. I had more questions than answers. I wondered whether Wade was safe in Afghanistan and if Lawrence would make it through the semester before the authorities pulled up in a white van and took him to a padded cell. I would graduate from high school in a few months but had no sense of a plan for the future or how I could possibly rebuild my dream of playing basketball at the college level.

I wallowed through my first three classes before Rebecca tracked me down. She had a knack for being everywhere all the time, especially those times when I didn't want to see her. This time she was waiting for me outside our fourth-period science class. "How'd it go with Stretch's dad?"

"Not good," I said.

I explained to Rebecca how Stretch's dad had a lot riding on the warehouse job and couldn't take a chance on a rookie crew working unsupervised in the dead of night. "Mr. Puckett said he wanted to help us out, but he just couldn't."

"So that's it? You're giving up?"

Oh, brother. Everything was caving in around me, and now the girl I sort of liked was questioning my intestinal fortitude. I didn't know what she expected me to say.

"What was I supposed to do? He said no."

Rebecca did her stare-off-into-space thing up until the bell rang for the start of fourth period. She shrugged and moved toward the classroom but then stopped short and turned around. "You're Ezekiel Archer. You can do anything you set your mind to."

If Rebecca meant that as encouragement, it didn't work. It only made me feel worse. "Sometimes your expectations of people are too high," I said.

Rebecca didn't respond. She took her seat in science class and sat in silence for the entire period, her brown bangs shielding her eyes from view. I holed up at a desk on the other side of the room, wondering if I'd let her down. Or was it my friends I'd let down? Or myself? It felt like the classroom walls were closing in.

When the lunch bell rang, Rebecca left the room and walked in the opposite direction from the cafeteria. I caught up with Curtis and Stretch inside, but there wasn't much to talk about. Everything had already been said. I gazed over at Lawrence's table. He was there, as usual, meeting his nutritional needs from the contents of a foil bag. He was a model of predictability at a time when so much was going on that I could not understand nor explain.

Curtis and Stretch and I said our goodbyes. I left the cafeteria for fifth-period journalism, stopping by Lawrence's table to check in. When I arrived, I noticed something was different. "What's going on?"

Lawrence's pocket protector was in its usual spot in his shirt pocket, but his pencils, all seven of them, were splayed out on the table, interconnected in a heptagonal shape. "I'm unscrambling their signal," he said.

I was beginning to take comfort in Lawrence's consistent level of advanced gibberish. I still had a couple of minutes before my next class, so I probed deeper. "Why are you doing that?"

He wrote me another note:

> *They found out I've been intercepting and decoding their communiqués, so they altered their spectral broadcast subcarrier to a non-neutral linear half-frequency.*

Lawrence and I didn't make eye contact, but he must have sensed my blank expression and wrote another note:

> *I'll translate that. They changed the channel. I'm adjusting my antenna.*

"Good luck with that."

I went through the motions the rest of the day at school and went home. There was a note from my mom saying she was working late again. I had homework to do but wasn't in the mood to do it. It was Friday night. That meant there was a college basketball game on the regional network, but when

I flipped the TV to that channel, there was only static. Add another basketball irregularity to the growing list.

I laid down on the couch and closed my eyes. I must have fallen asleep, because the doorbell rang and startled me. My watch read 11:30 p.m.

"Who's there?" I looked through the peephole and saw the naval-to-armpit midsection of a tall person.

"It's me, Stretch."

I opened the door. "What are you doing here? Is something wrong?"

"Only if you've made other plans tonight and can't come with us," said Stretch, standing in stained coveralls that were way too short.

"Who's 'us'?"

"We are us, I mean, I am them . . . wait, they are we." Stretch was too excited to make any sense.

"Slow down, big fella. What's going on?"

"Grab your gear, soldier, and fall in," he said.

I laced up my high-tops and locked the door behind me. When we got to the bottom of the stairs, I saw it. I staggered backward and stared.

"I know, she's a beauty, right?"

It was Mr. Puckett's van. I could tell because the words PUCKETT PAINTING were stenciled onto the side. There were ladders draped across the top, and Curtis was behind the wheel—Curtis, as in the only one of us who had a driver's license. Stretch's dad had drunk one beer too many with dinner, and that was the break we needed.

"Are you out of your mind?"

"We'll have it back by daybreak," Stretch said. "Get in."

There was that feeling rolling over me again. I had felt it most recently at Jefferson Community College when we signed up for the tournament. Hope made another unexpected appearance. I swung open the side cargo door to find several five-gallon buckets of paint, paintbrushes, rollers and poles, and a box of drop cloths. And Rebecca. She was sitting cross-legged on the van floor, wearing a turned-around painter's cap and smiling.

"I suppose you're responsible for this," I said. It was the second time in as many days Rebecca had beaten me to a great idea.

"I know how much that goofy tournament means to you jocks," she said. "Couldn't just sit around and let Brock Decker's team have all the fun."

As Curtis piloted Mr. Puckett's van across the city, I wondered how we would paint the entire warehouse and make it to Jefferson by nine in the morning. Then there was the matter of competing in the tournament on no sleep.

For that moment, though, I was just happy to be with my friends.

9

Remember Not to Slug Anybody

It was midnight. Curtis pulled the van up to the guard shack of an industrial complex in a sketchy part of the city.

"Dude, are you sure this is it?" Curtis asked Stretch, our designated navigator for the covert operation.

"Yep, this is it. 12501 Erving Causeway. There's the sign. Consolidated Enterprises."

Curtis hand-cranked the window down as a uniformed guard, armed with a flashlight and a clipboard, approached our van. "You gentlemen lost?" he asked.

Curtis dropped his voice a full octave in an attempt to sound older. "No, sir. We're with Puckett Painting. Got a contract to paint the inside of a warehouse."

The guard perused a list on his clipboard. "Puckett, right?"

"Right," Curtis said. "This is Mr. Puckett over here." Curtis motioned to Stretch, who half-saluted the guard. Stretch, thankfully, was in the shadows on the other side of the van, and I hoped all the guard could see was a big guy who could have been Mr. Puckett.

The guard examined his paperwork more thoroughly. He wrinkled his forehead and looked up at Curtis. "You're not supposed to be here until morning."

Curtis was quick to respond. "Yes, I know. We're early."

The guard didn't budge. "The schedule says eight a.m. I can't let you in until then. Back it up, gentlemen."

Rebecca's lower lip curled. My heart sank. Curtis reached for the gearshift, but his forearm was met by Stretch's hand before he could put the van into reverse.

Stretch leaned forward in his seat and cleared his throat. "Excuse me, young man." Stretch was at least twenty years younger than the guard. "I don't think you understand. We've got a contract to paint that warehouse. We're here early because we've got a busy schedule. If you don't let us in there tonight, that warehouse will not get painted." Stretch paused before delivering the dagger: "And that's going to be on you, son."

Uh-oh. Stretch had just "sonned" the security guard. Rebecca covered her mouth with her hands. Curtis remained frozen. I could feel the blood drain from my face. We were going to the slammer, I knew it.

The guard scoured the contents of his clipboard one final time before turning to Stretch and giving him a death stare. "Park it over there."

Curtis rolled his window back up. He maneuvered through

a maze of trucks and light poles before parking the van in the warehouse's loading zone. He threw the gearshift into park, cut the lights and ignition, and punched Stretch in the arm.

"What's that for?"

"General principle, dude," Curtis said. "At least this isn't your shooting arm."

I looked at my watch. We had less than nine hours to paint the entire warehouse, take the van back to Stretch's place, and get to Jefferson for the start of the tournament.

Stretch opened the roll-up door to the warehouse. The vast space was empty, but there were walls everywhere and no time to spare, so we wasted no time unloading the van.

Stretch, the seasoned junior contractor, divvied up our responsibilities. That meant Curtis and I would do the heavy lifting, Rebecca would be in charge of paint-bucket logistics, and Stretch would boss everyone around.

After an hour, we were exhausted and our nostrils stung from the acrid paint fumes. By the time we finished, just before eight in the morning, we were covered in paint and could barely stand.

Stretch did a final inspection while the rest of us loaded up the van. Curtis started the engine, Rebecca climbed into the back, and I went inside to get Stretch. I found the big man looking up at a wall as if he were examining fine art in a museum, an elbow resting on the palm of one hand, the other hand supporting his chin. Stretch shook his head in disapproval. "I think you missed a spot."

"Get in the van now."

Curtis retraced our path out of the parking lot, but when

we got to the gate, it was padlocked and the guard was gone. Curtis honked the horn, but the place was a ghost town. We were stranded.

Stretch got out of the van and opened the rear door, poking around until he found a weathered pair of bolt cutters. He walked over to the gate and snapped off the padlock like a pretzel. “A painter is like a private eye,” he said. “He’s got to be quick on his feet and ready for anything.”

So do an astronaut and a bus driver, but Stretch had always wanted to be an undercover agent. He helped out his dad on the job because he felt a family obligation. Mr. Puckett would love nothing better than for his son to take over the family business. But I knew Stretch wanted to make his mark on the world in a career that did not involve a paint roller. As difficult as it was to imagine a six-foot-ten PI blending into the scenery as a disinterested third party while investigating suspected criminal activity, I wanted him to know he could count on me for moral support.

“C’mon, Sherlock Holmes, let’s get out of here.” That was all the support I had left in me after my all-nighter as his personal assistant.

Curtis gave it gas and we took off. Thirty minutes later, he parked the van in front of Stretch’s house. “I’ll see you guys at the college,” he said as he disappeared down the street.

Rebecca jumped out of the van, her blue jeans caked with blotches of white paint. “I appreciate what you did for us,” I told her. “It really means a lot to me.”

“Good luck out there today,” she said before giving me a quick hug. “Remember not to slug anybody.” The girl had a sense of humor. I liked that about her.

I ran the short distance to my apartment and was able to change into my basketball clothes without waking Mom. Then I pedaled my bike to Jefferson in a race against time. I was tired, but there was basketball on the horizon. I arrived the same time as Curtis, ten minutes till go time. We were only missing a basketball, eight hours of sleep, and Stretch.

Curtis and I went inside the gym. There were dozens of kids in uniforms warming up and shooting around. I saw Coach Kincaid at the registration table giving instructions to the people working the event. He looked up at the wall clock and so did I. It was 8:55.

We didn't have a basketball, so we took a few laps around the gym to get loose. I hadn't shot a ball for days, so I had no idea what would happen when I threw up my first jumper.

Coach Kincaid concluded his business at the registration table and took a sweeping look around the gym. He smiled when he saw us, but that smile faded when he realized that Curtis and I were one big man short of a team.

The clock on the wall clicked over to 9:00. Coach Kincaid stepped to center court and told the event volunteers standing at the gym's entrance to close the doors. It was the coach's version of a tardy lockout.

"Good morning, everyone. Welcome to Jefferson Community College's first annual three-on-three basketball tournament. I'm Coach Kincaid. Let's get this thing underway."

I knew Coach Kincaid was disappointed, because I could feel it from across the gym. If there had been a hole in the court, I would have crawled inside.

10

Rock and Fire

What happened next was a blur. I looked up at the clock in disbelief. It was still nine o'clock, straight up. Coach Kincaid addressed the referees and the dozens of players. I caught a glimpse of Curtis, who looked as though his dog had been hit by a bus. I scanned the bleachers searching for, I didn't know, maybe Wade, or my dad, or a miracle.

Nothing.

Then I heard someone banging on the gym's double doors. All eyes turned toward those doors, except mine. I was watching the clock. Still 9:00. Someone pushed the metal bar to unlatch the door. Stretch walked through and bent over to catch his breath, hands resting on his knees.

I swiveled my head to Coach Kincaid, who looked at the clock. Still 9:00. It was the longest sixty seconds in the history of time. I saw Stretch out of the corner of my eye gasping for air. I took one more look at the clock. It was 9:01.

We were in.

Curtis and I sidled over to the gasping Stretch.

"Dude, what happened?" Curtis said.

Stretch took a couple gulps of air. "My dad . . ."

"What about him?" Curtis said.

"He was really pissed. He lectured me on responsibility and maturity and stuff. When I noticed it was eight forty-five, I asked if he could possibly finish the lecture later. He smiled and wished me good luck."

Coach Kincaid was doing some lecturing of his own as he laid out the tournament rules. Thirty-two teams would pair off against one another on the college's eight half-courts. The tournament was single elimination, meaning that if we lost a game, we'd watch the rest of the event from the cheap seats.

The scoring rules were simple. Baskets made from inside the three-point arc would count as one point—not two, as in regular team play. Baskets made from beyond the three-point line would only count as two points—no three-pointers. Free throws were worth one point apiece, as usual.

"First team to twenty points is the winner, and there is no win-by-two rule," Coach Kincaid said. "The two teams that win all their games in the first four rounds will play on the main court for the tournament championship." Coach Kincaid concluded by reminding everyone about rule number five: "We expect good sportsmanship from all of you, especially the team captains."

Coach didn't look my way when he said it, but I knew that final comment was aimed at me. It was hard to blame him.

I took a moment to check out the competition and noticed that all the other teams were wearing handsome matching uniforms.

Not us.

Curtis had on a headband to keep his shaggy hair out of his eyes, plus a Hawaiian shirt with the sleeves cut off, board shorts, and deck shoes. Yes, deck shoes. Curtis reasoned that they helped him to move his feet more efficiently when he was trying to get open beyond the arc. With shooting skills like his, who were we to argue?

Stretch wore a tank top that advertised the painting business, swimming trunks, and size 18 basketball shoes, the kind with a lot of colored stripes and plastic stuff on them. Stretch contended they made him look cool, a point Curtis and I challenged him on from time to time.

I wore my trusty reversible practice jersey, a pair of Chip's Sporting Goods house-brand game shorts, my good-luck floppy socks, and black high-tops.

It felt as if we were underdressed sophomores at the school dance.

"Security!" Every unpleasant experience in my life included Brock Decker, who was approaching. "Hey, dweeb. I'm surprised they let you in the gym."

Brock was flanked by Thatcher and Duncan, two of his former teammates from Mid-City Prep. Thatcher and Duncan were also linebackers on Mid-City Prep's football team. I theorized that they played basketball for the opportunity to push smaller kids around.

"Great to see you," I said, taking the high road. "Good luck today."

"See if you can manage to win a few games so me and my bodyguards can have that rematch," Brock said. I remembered overhearing Brock telling his buddies at McDerney that Coach Kincaid had granted him an exception, allowing him to represent Mid-City Prep in the tournament.

"We'll work on that." I'd played enough games of basketball to know the importance of dealing with the task in front of us. By doing so, the future would take care of itself.

An event volunteer posted the team rosters and court assignments as I gathered my teammates for a pregame strategy session. Stretch would set screens at the high post and patrol the boards. Curtis, our long-range sharpshooter, would roam the exterior hardwood in search of open looks. My job was to run the floor on offense and call out picks on defense.

As team captain, the responsibility to fire up the team fell on my shoulders. "We've done this a million times. Let's just do what we do and go home," I said. "Curtis, the more times you can drill it from downtown, the quicker we move on."

I wasn't kidding about that. We were playing on no sleep and little food. This was not a day to let the other team hang around. We shook hands with our first opponents, a team from Rolling Valley High, before losing the coin toss to determine which squad would have first possession. No surprise there. Nothing was going to be easy. Ball out to Rolling Valley.

The game got underway, and we were down 7–0 before we knew what hit us. Stretch was getting pushed around under the basket. Curtis couldn't find his rhythm from distance. I lost the ball out of bounds every time I put it on the deck.

"Timeout, ref." Teams were allowed one timeout per game. I needed to use ours to settle us down.

Curtis hung his head and muttered something to himself. Stretch sat down on the sideline, toweled off his face, and downed an entire liter of water. I was so exhausted, my legs wobbled.

"You fellas okay?"

"We're good, Coach." That response, those three words, took whatever strength I had left. If Coach Kincaid had asked a follow-up question, I would have just stared at him. He went back to the registration table and took his seat.

I turned to Curtis and said the first thing that came into my mind. "Rock and fire, kid, hit the glove!" The guys looked at me as though I'd lost my mind. I was so weary, maybe I had. "Make him hit your pitch. Just play catch. Don't give into him." I rattled off every phrase a softball coach would say to a pitcher who was on the ropes. I wanted to keep going, but I ran out of breath and phrases.

"Medic!" Stretch tried to bring me back to earth. "Zeke—*Zeke!* You good?"

I regained my senses as the referee blew his whistle to signal the end of the timeout. Stretch and I were dog-tired. Curtis seemed physically fine but was having a crisis of confidence. I put my hands on his shoulders and looked him in the eye. "Just pretend we're at the center playing horse," I told him.

"I've seen you shoot the lights out of every gym in L.A. County. You're Curtis Short. You can do this."

It must have worked.

Stretch and I did everything we could to get Curtis the ball. He put on a shooting clinic, canning one long-range jumper after another. He hit seven in a row from distance before a small crowd gathered to bear witness. When Curtis buried his tenth straight to close it out, 20–7, Stretch reached down to give him a high five while I looked for the nearest bench and collapsed.

One down, four to go. No way I had enough in the tank to keep going.

11

Rub Some Dirt on It and Walk It Off

"Zeke!"

I opened my eyes. I was flat on my back on the ground. Stretch was standing over me. I knew it had to be Stretch, because I didn't know anyone else as tall and geeky-looking.

"They're calling us for the next game. C'mon, man, get up!"

I must have passed out. I remembered Curtis raining two-balls on a bewildered trio from Rolling Valley, but that was it.

Curtis and Stretch each extended a hand and pulled me to my feet. I felt dizzy and my mouth was parched. Stretch handed me a bottle of water with half its contents already gone. I knew I had come to my senses, because I asked the big man whether he had drunk the other half.

"No way, I found it like that," Stretch said. His grin told me otherwise, but my survival instinct kicked in and I drank it anyway.

Curtis handed me a towel and a scouting report on our next opponent, Western Charter High. "I watched their first game while you were napping. They're quick, bro, but they don't have anyone taller than five nine."

That was all Stretch needed to hear. "I've got this one," he said.

Stretch was used to trading elbows with players who were often wider and sometimes as tall, but this was a rare opportunity to use his size to flat-out dominate. He didn't say it, but he knew he had to carry the team on his back until I got my second wind. If ever there were a time to exploit Stretch's height, this was it.

"Just get me the ball," he said.

Curtis and I took turns lobbing it into the post. Stretch either banked home a hook shot or kicked it out to one of us for an easy midrange jumper. At one point, the players from Western Charter tried to triple-team the Tall One, but that only hastened their departure from the tournament.

"I'm looking forward to you rookies trying that low-post garbage on us." Brock and his friends had wandered over to watch our second game after winning theirs, and Brock felt the need to weigh in on our strategy.

"Beat it, Decker." Curtis was not in the mood for Brock's wise-guy antics.

"I seem to remember doing some effective laundry hanging against that scarecrow not too long ago," Brock said.

Curtis glared at Brock and took a step toward him. I was too tired to break it up, but Coach Kincaid wasn't. "You gentlemen had better find a way to share the same space, right now, or it's going to be an early exit for all of you." Coach Kincaid didn't want a repeat in his gym of what had happened in the city championship. "Wouldn't it make a lot more sense to settle your differences peacefully on the court?"

"Sorry, sir," I said.

Coach Kincaid carried a look of disappointment back to the registration table.

"Sounds good to me, if you guys make it that far," Brock said.

I didn't know what Brock meant by that, so I went to where the rosters and court assignments were posted to scan the brackets. There it was: the way the tournament was set up, Brock's team and ours couldn't meet until the finals—only after winning four games each.

"We need to hold it together," I said to Curtis. "It's really important."

Curtis crossed his arms. "Dude" was all he said, but I knew he was unhappy.

"You have to express that with a basketball in your hands."

Curtis looked away. He wasn't buying it, so I tried a different approach. "Can't you see he's trying to get into your head? Maybe he's jealous of our awesome chemistry and secretly wants to join our team."

Curtis chuckled and threw his hands into the air. "I give, dude. Brock's really a gnarly guy. Maybe he's free for burgers after the tourney."

"Atta kid."

A referee blew his whistle to signal the start of the third round. By then, I had most of my strength back, and I could tell that Curtis and Stretch did as well. The matchups got tougher the deeper into the tournament we went. Next on the roster was Hillview High. When they took the court, I did a double take. No, make that a triple take.

"Those are the Havershim triplets. Don, Von, and Ron. As identical as they come," Curtis said. "I've heard about these guys. A biological near impossibility, but a scary basketball reality. They run a crazy three-man weave. Old school."

The three-man weave is a motion offense that involves a lot of passing and cutting to the basket. It's easy to defend under normal circumstances. But factor in our need to conserve energy, and the triplets spelled trouble.

"Who do you want to guard?" Stretch asked as he tried to conceal a smile.

"I'm thinking about slugging you on the arm right now, but I'm not sure I have enough strength to hit you as hard as I want to," Curtis said.

"Doesn't much matter," I said. "Take whoever guards you."

After we lost the coin toss for the third time in a row, the Havershim triplets dazzled their way to an early 6–2 lead. By the time they extended it to 13–5, we were spent.

"Timeout, ref."

We couldn't keep up. It was like playing Whac-a-Mole. One of the Havershims was always wide open and streaking toward the basket. We had to make an adjustment or get bounced from the tournament.

"We're switching to a zone," I said.

The zone defense is the basketball equivalent to the Zen proverb, "It's never too late to do nothing." I handed out the defensive assignments. Stretch would camp out in the paint, Curtis and I would plant ourselves on the wings, and we'd wait for the Havershims to burn themselves out.

Play resumed and the Havershims ran the weave. Then they ran it some more. When one of them cut to the basket, Stretch stepped forward and blocked the shot. We took them out of their element, and in doing so, we exposed their fatal weakness: poor outside shooting.

While the trio tossed up one brick after another, Curtis got hot and Stretch pounded the boards. We hammered the Havershims, 20–13, and rested up for the fourth round.

"How are you guys feeling?" I asked as the next whistle loomed.

"My feet are killing me," Stretch said, "but at least they look good inside these boats."

Curtis took off his sweatband, closed his eyes, and ran his hand through his wet hair. I'd seen him do that before a big game to draw his focus inward. Curtis knew we'd look to get him open in our next game, and he understood how critical it was that his shot find its way home. That would open up the inside for Stretch and give me more choices with the ball.

"Earth to Curtis, come in." That was my way of reeling Curtis back.

He opened his eyes. "I see the future," he said. "I see a look of disappointment on Brock Decker's face. I see hardware, a trophy, perhaps. Dude, it is our destiny."

Curtis was ready. Stretch, too. It was a good thing, because the pressure was mounting. There were only three other teams still alive, including Brock's crew and our next opponent, three ballers from Riverton High.

We matched up well with Riverton. I knew it would be a war. This time we won the coin flip. We had first possession.

I inbounded the ball to Stretch at the high post. He passed it back to me and I dished it off to a wide-open Curtis on the wing. Curtis would ordinarily take the shot, but he decided instead to throw a fake and go hard to the rim. He went up for a layup, and I watched in horror as he rolled his right ankle on his opponent's foot on the way down.

His ankle made a sound I haven't forgotten. We had a 1–0 lead, and one-third of our team was lying on the floor in agony.

The ref blew his whistle. "Officials' timeout."

Curtis's ankle swelled up. It looked as though he was concealing a golf ball inside his sock. A tournament volunteer ran to retrieve a bag of ice.

Curtis sat up, a look of worry radiating across his face. "Is it bad, dude?"

"Nah, just a scratch," Stretch said. "Rub some dirt on it and walk it off."

Stretch was trying to keep the moment light, but Curtis was in bad shape, and our chances of advancing to the championship round were fading fast.

12

Dude, It's Basketball . . . It's Always Worth It

It was one of those times when deck shoes were not the best choice of footwear for competitive basketball. Those shoes enabled Curtis to move more freely than high-tops, but their construction offered minimal ankle support.

Coach Kincaid, as a precautionary measure, had arranged for medical personnel to attend the event. The coach escorted an older gentleman with a medical bag to where Curtis had fallen.

"Young man, I'm Dr. Binder," he said. "Let's take a look."

Dr. Binder bent down on one knee to examine Curtis's ankle, which was already black and blue. When the doctor tried to flex it, Curtis bit down hard on his hand and let out a muffled scream.

"I don't think it's broken," the doctor said, "but it looks like a nasty sprain. I'd like to take that shoe off and get a closer look."

"No, dude," said Curtis in protest. "Just get me an ice pack. I'll be fine."

I sat down next to Curtis and rested my hand on his back. "What do you think, bud?"

"I think if he takes off my shoe, everything's going to swell up, and I'm never gonna get it back on."

There was a glimmer of hope in those words. If Curtis wanted to keep his shoe on, it meant he intended to keep playing regardless of what his ankle was telling him. I saw the referee talking with Coach Kincaid, who wore a look of concession on his face. Then the ref came back to Curtis.

"I'm sorry, son, but the rules call for a five-minute injury assessment period. If you can't go back on the court by now, I'll have no choice but to declare the game a forfeit."

Tournament regulations did not allow for teams to compete with only two players, which was fine, because Riverton would have creamed Stretch and me in a game of three-on-two.

"Dude, help me up," Curtis said.

Stretch and I pulled our friend to his feet. Curtis winced as he flexed his ankle. I couldn't tell whether the tears in his eyes were from pain or the anguish of advancing so far in the tournament only to forfeit in the semifinals. "I'm good. Let's go."

I wasn't sure Curtis was making the right decision. "I don't know, man, you might make it worse. It's not worth it."

Curtis hobbled around, testing the limits of what he could do on the court. "Gimme the ball," he said.

The ref bounced the game ball to Curtis. He pivoted toward the basket on his good ankle, bounced the ball a few times, and threw up a twenty-five-foot rainbow.

Nothing but net.

Curtis motioned me over to where he was standing. "Dude, it's basketball," he whispered. "It's always worth it."

The ref blew his whistle to signal the resumption of play as I huddled the team together. "Let's go zone defense again. That'll slow the game down." I poked the big man in the chest. "Run pick and roll, I'll look for you underneath." Not wanting to show favoritism, I poked Curtis in the chest too. "Okay, tough guy, give us what you got."

I thought if we played conservatively and went basket-for-basket with Riverton, it would buy enough time for Curtis to work through the pain. The longer the game went on, the more his adrenaline took over and masked the damage. Our opponent tried to overload Curtis's side of the zone to take advantage of his limited mobility, but Stretch and I adjusted on defense and shut down the passing lanes.

When Riverton's point guard whirled around Curtis and scored a bucket that tied the score at 18–18, I waved the guys over.

"How is it?" I asked Curtis.

"Trying not to think about it, dude," he said.

I realized the Riverton players weren't worrying about Curtis, because they thought he wasn't a threat. They were taking advantage of his injury by double-teaming Stretch near the basket and would release a man to cover Curtis only if he was in range when we kicked the ball out to him.

Everyone in the gym knew that Curtis could barely move, but only Stretch and I were aware that as long as he was upright, he was hands down the best shooter in the tournament.

I called the next play. "Backcourt loner."

I based the name on the definition of the word *loner*, a person who prefers to be alone, which was how Curtis needed to be in the backcourt for us to close out Riverton.

The ref resumed play. Curtis, standing a few feet in front of the half-court stripe, inbounded the ball and stood there. Stretch and I worked the ball toward the basket to collapse the defense, leaving Curtis wide open but too far away to be a scoring threat.

Or so it seemed to Riverton.

I kicked the ball out to an unguarded Curtis, who took a one-bounce dribble and rattled home a forty-foot rainmaker that rolled up the sidewalks in game four.

We were in the finals.

Coach Kincaid stepped to center court, this time to thank all the participants who were not advancing. "We truly appreciate your support," he said. "I hope you can stick around for the championship game between our two finalists, representing Mid-City Prep and McDerney Continuation. We'll tip it off in thirty minutes."

I heard a familiar voice behind me. "I think I can hang around for that." I turned around to find Rebecca. I didn't expect to see her there. "Made you guys some lunch," she said. "Thought you might be hungry."

Legend had it that Stretch had never in his life missed a meal up to that point, and history was not about to be made that afternoon—not in the *food* department anyway. Curtis thought that if he ate something, it might take his mind off his injury. I wasn't hungry but understood at some deeper level that I needed sustenance.

"What's in the bag?" Stretch said.

"Let me see. I made you a peanut-butter-and-jelly sandwich. Curtis, cream cheese and sliced pickles on white bread, hold the crust, right? Ezekiel, looks like this one's yours. American cheese on egg bread with square-ended carrot spears. Miss anyone?"

Not hardly. It wasn't enough that her idea of painting the warehouse overnight had saved the day. Then she showed up with our favorite meals when we needed them most.

"You bring napkins?" That was Stretch's way of saying thanks. We were all grateful for Rebecca's kindness. I wasn't used to having anyone look after me like that. It felt good.

Rebecca turned her attention to Curtis. "Not going to ask if it hurts, like some people." She looked over at me and did her gigantic eye-roll thing. "Can you move it?"

Curtis leaned forward to adjust the ice pack Dr. Binder had handed him the second we had stepped off the court. "Not much."

Rebecca knelt down and examined Curtis's ankle. "Mind if I try something?"

"Yes, I mind."

None of us knew what Rebecca had in mind, but with the title game twenty minutes away, I was willing to try anything. "Do you know what you're doing?" As soon as those words left my mouth, I wished I could take them back.

"Guess you don't really know me."

That was true, but how could I? When I'd walked Rebecca home two days earlier, I asked how she'd ended up at McDerney but didn't get an answer. "So fill me in," I said.

"Not really much to explain," Rebecca said. "Studying sports medicine. Just learned about soft-tissue injuries. This ankle needs rest, ice, compression, and elevation: RICE. Rest is not an option at the moment, but the other three are."

Rebecca went to the first aid station next to the registration table and asked for a roll of elastic bandage. We watched as she used the techniques she had learned in school to create localized pressure on Curtis's ankle with a compression wrap. When she finished, she draped the ice pack back over the ankle and propped up Curtis's leg on a chair to help reduce the swelling. Curtis grimaced throughout but otherwise survived.

Then another familiar but less welcome voice broke the silence.

"Press agent and now team doctor. Impressive skill set."

"Go away, Brock," I said.

"I'm really hoping you guys won't have to forfeit," Brock said. "I could use the exercise."

With that, Brock went to hang with Thatcher and Duncan. I didn't have to tell Brock a second time to back off. That made me think he might be concerned about how his team would stack up against ours.

We rested together on the hardwood, brothers in arms plus one sister, as the game clock counted down to zero. Getting this far into the tournament was something I'd never thought would happen. I took comfort in surrounding myself with my closest friends as the moment approached.

I surveyed the crowd that had gathered in the bleachers. The rec center's director, Mr. Shields, was there. So was Chip Spears. I recognized a few high school players I'd gone up against while I attended Southland Central. I tried not to let the moment overwhelm me, but it was a struggle. The game would be the biggest of my life.

The horn sounded. Coach Kincaid walked to center court and welcomed everyone in attendance as Rebecca hurried to find a seat in the stands.

"What a great day of basketball it's been," the coach said.

Coach Kincaid ran through the tournament rules again, with special emphasis on rule number five and good sportsmanship. By then, it was clear that rule number five was his personal favorite. He took his time as he made the point one final time. Then Coach Kincaid introduced the two referees who would officiate the game.

Curtis elbowed me in the ribs and whispered a question he already knew the answer to. "Dude, aren't those the two refs who . . . ?"

Always were, always would be.

I glanced at Stretch, who was staring bug-eyed into the rafters. Curtis was still talking, but for the life of me, I don't remember what he said. I looked at Coach Kincaid, who seemed interested in gauging my reaction. They were the same referees who had called our city-title game against Mid-City Prep. If there were any doubt, one of them still had a swollen jaw.

Someone was testing me. I recalled a conversation I'd had with Wade before he left for boot camp. We talked about fear and the importance of confronting it. "If you don't stand up to your fears, if you just walk away from them, they have a way of coming back to find you," Wade told me. I was too young to understand what he meant at the time, but I had a good idea as I stood there, because my fears had just walked onto the court wearing black-and-white striped shirts and whistles around their necks.

"Shake hands, gentlemen," Coach Kincaid said as we gathered at center court. When I reached out to greet the ref I had punched, he met my hand, squeezed hard, and didn't let go until I made it clear I wanted it back.

The guys and I went to the sideline for final preparations when I heard the other ref say something to Coach Kincaid.

"Coach, where's the game ball?"

The game ball had been sitting atop the registration table, but it was no longer there. In fact, an eerie silence had fallen in the gym: there were no basketballs bouncing anywhere—which was weird, because just moments earlier there'd been balls ringing off the hardwood all over the place.

I wondered what Lawrence would say if he were sitting at a table in the gym having lunch. It would probably be something about how the decision to rid the world of basketball had advanced to the next level, and I was the person responsible.

Coach Kincaid motioned for Mr. Shields to come down to the court. They spoke for a moment before the coach handed him a set of keys. Mr. Shields left the gym and returned a couple of minutes later with a basketball.

The ball was flat and dusty. I recognized it from the photo I'd seen in Coach Kincaid's office when I signed up for the tournament. It was the championship game ball from twenty-five years ago, when Mr. Shields was head coach at Jefferson. Now it was the only ball left in the building, and Lawrence was probably the only person around who could explain why it had been spared.

Mr. Shields took a hand pump from an event volunteer and pumped life back into that basketball. The referees tested the ball, and somehow it held its air after sitting idle for so many years.

"Tails." Brock made his decision as a referee flipped a silver dollar into the air. I watched the coin descend end-over-end back toward earth as I thought about the decision I had made at the city finals, less random than a coin flip but with consequences far greater.

"Tails it is."

We were behind the eight ball, and we hadn't even touched the basketball.

13

Let's Get the Bucket and Go Home

I huddled Curtis and Stretch together. "Take who takes you."

Thatcher was nearly as tall as Stretch, and Duncan was smart and quick like Curtis, so those matchups were set. That left Brock to guard me. It was the only way I wanted it.

"Play smart and protect the ball," I told the guys. "Let's keep our heads—we've come too far to do anything stupid." That last bit of advice was more for me than the two chums standing in front of me.

Brock tried to inbound the basketball to Duncan, but I deflected it and Curtis picked up the loose ball. He fired a pass to Stretch, who took it to the hoop in full stride. Stretch was met there by Thatcher, who went up to block Stretch's shot but instead knocked the big man to the deck.

The refs blew their whistles. Brock and I took a step toward Thatcher and Stretch but stopped short. Coach Kincaid stood up from his seat.

"Foul!" shouted a ref, as if he were trying to restore order prior to sending Stretch to the free-throw line. Cooler heads prevailed and Stretch, bruised and rattled, air-balled his first free throw.

"C'mon, pitch and catch, hit the glove," I said.

The ref tossed Stretch the ball for the second of two from the stripe. Stretch sank it to give us a 1–0 lead.

Curtis had regained some mobility in his ankle, which meant he could move more freely on the perimeter, and that opened up the inside for Stretch and me to run pick and rolls on offense and keep Brock's crew off the boards on defense. I hadn't seen Brock play since the city championship. His game had improved in that short amount of time. It was all I could do to contain him when he had the ball. I tried to overplay his right hand, but he went to his left more fluidly than I remembered.

Fatigue set in as the cumulative effect of no sleep and little food took its toll. We traded baskets and kept the score close, tying it at 17–17 on a hook shot from Stretch in the lane. Brock called a timeout. I took my team's pulse as Brock and his teammates went into pre-celebration mode.

"You guys okay?" I asked.

"Really hurts, dude," Curtis said. "Don't have much left. May have to amputate."

"I can help you with that. I haven't got much going on after the game." I guessed Stretch was feeling all right. That made one of us, because I felt lightheaded and dizzy.

"What's the plan, bro?" Curtis operated best when we knew in advance what we were going to do.

"Yeah, what about it?" Stretch said.

I had no idea how we were going to survive the game, let alone win it, and the guys were counting on me to come up with a miracle. I toweled beads of sweat from my forehead and took a long drink of water. "Let's switch to man-to-man defense."

That decision was met with puzzled looks. There were advantages to playing a man defense, but conserving strength wasn't one of them.

"I don't know, dude," Curtis said. "Don't think I can guard that guy. He's too quick. I can't move."

"I think it'll work," I said, even though I had my doubts. "They won't be expecting it, so we'll catch them off guard. Just get in Duncan's face and stay there for as long as you can. Stretch and I will help you out."

The ref blew his whistle to resume play. Brock inbounded the ball to Duncan, who faked Curtis out of his board shorts and drained a two-pointer that put us on the edge of losing: 19–17. One more point and they'd win. Curtis hung his head. I couldn't tell if he was exhausted or embarrassed.

"Shake it off, kid," I whispered. "Next one's coming to you."

I wasted no time inbounding the ball to Curtis and hustled to set a screen on Duncan. Curtis saw the play developing. He threw a jab-step fake off his good ankle, leaned back, and knocked down a two-point fall-away from distance to knot it at 19–19.

"Atta kid!" I said.

"Lucky shot, gimpy," Brock said.

We needed to make a stop, or Brock would punch his own ticket to the Sunflower State. He inbounded the ball to Thatcher and called for it back. Brock was determined to put us out of our misery all by himself as he yo-yoed the dribble and looked for daylight.

I overplayed his left side, which invited him to use his strong hand to take the ball to the rim. What Brock didn't realize was that I was leading him right into Stretch, and the big man tomahawked Brock's shot in the opposite direction. I went horizontal and dove for the loose ball, my body bouncing hard off the deck.

"Timeout, ref!" I bellowed.

"I think I got a piece of that one," Stretch said as he sauntered to the sideline.

I knew we had only one chance left, because we were running on fumes. I thought about drawing up some sort of razzmatazz play, but my instincts told me to stick with the fundamentals. I rested my hand on Curtis's shoulder. "Take your guy out on the elbow and keep him there. They're afraid of your shot, so let's let them think you're going to put it up."

The ref blew his whistle. "Let's go, gentlemen."

I looked up at Stretch—with Stretch, I was always looking up. I had never seen such confidence in his eyes. "It's you and me, big man. Set a high-post pick. I'll run Brock through it and look for a pass from Curtis. Let's get the bucket and go home."

Stretch tried to keep it light. "I've always wanted to visit Kansas in the springtime."

14

Is He Alive?

I inbounded the ball to Curtis on the left wing. Stretch camped out in the low post, drawing Thatcher down with him. I stood above the two-point line at the top of the key and passed the ball back and forth with Curtis. When it seemed like we'd lulled the defense into a false sense of security, I glanced over to Stretch and gave him the look, a combination nod and raised eyebrow. It was part of the basketball code we'd developed from years together on the court.

Stretch darted for the high post at the corner of the key as I threw the ball to Curtis. Curtis faked the shot as I broke for the basket. Stretch steadied himself for contact as I ran Brock into the screen. Brock slammed hard into Stretch and hit the floor as Curtis found me with a bounce pass in the lane.

Thatcher backpedaled and tried in vain to catch me. Using the backboard as a shield—basketball had a way of protecting me when I needed it to—I went behind the basket, emerged from the other side, and flipped up a reverse layup. The ball kissed off the glass and slid through the net.

Ballgame.

The crowd roared as I braced for the mini-shockwave that sweeps across a basketball court when fans erupt as one. Stretch hopped up and down like a nine-year-old who got a pogo stick for Christmas. Curtis dropped to his knees and sobbed into his towel. My ears tingled from the sound of hands clapping. The stands were nowhere near as full as they had been at the city-title game, but it didn't matter. I could not contain the smile that overtook me.

I searched for a familiar face and found Rebecca's. I blinked once and locked my eyes onto hers. Rebecca spoke volumes to me in that moment, although no words were exchanged between us.

I came back to reality and noticed Brock still on the floor, dazed and beaten. I extended a hand to help him up. Brock stared at me for what seemed like a hundred years before extending his arm and locking his hand onto mine. I pulled him to his feet.

"Nice game."

"Good game, dweeb."

After a brief awards ceremony, where Coach Kincaid handed out plaques to Brock's team and mine, I went to the sideline to gather my gym bag and water bottle as people walked by to offer congratulations on their way out the door.

Chip Spears was the first person to approach. "Those other teams wore much nicer uniforms." Chip winked after he said that. I was glad to see he'd regained his sense of humor after what had happened at his store. I was about to ask him what the latest development was, but he beat me to it. "We never figured out what happened to all the basketball equipment, but I'll have twice as much gear in stock when we hold our grand reopening next week. You should stop by."

I still needed a new ball and was holding off buying it from Global Mega-Sports. "Sure thing, Chip. You can count on it."

Mr. Shields made his way down the bleachers and walked directly toward me. "Spirited effort, young man. Top shelf. I'm proud of you boys."

"Thanks, Mr. Shields." I had a lot of respect for Mr. Shields. He'd always given us the benefit of the doubt, even at those times when we might not have deserved it.

I was surprised to see Lawrence there. He was sitting alone in the top row at center court, pencil in hand, writing something on a notepad. Maybe he was keeping stats or needed a noisy place to do homework.

Another person approached to congratulate me, someone I did not expect to see at the tournament. "Excellent game plan, Ezekiel. Tactical, efficient, well executed." It was Vice Principal Littwack. I wondered if he'd come to the title game to see if Brock and I would behave ourselves.

"Thank you, sir. That means a lot coming from you."

As Mr. Littwack disappeared through the double doors, I thought about the irony of losing my athletic scholarship to the University of Kansas, only to end up about to travel there for a weekend tournament that at the moment seemed more like a chore than anything of real importance.

I thought about how proud I was of Curtis and Stretch, who had fought through pain, hunger, and exhaustion to help us win a tournament that I believed meant more to me than to them. I couldn't think of a better way to measure our friendship.

I considered how much I wished my brother had been there to see me play. I worried about his safety in a dangerous, far-off country on the other side of the globe. I thought about my mom, who I know wanted to be there but always had to work to keep up with our bills. I thought about how Rebecca had been a complete stranger just a few weeks before but had become a trusted friend—and perhaps more.

"That was a nifty play you drew up. Ever think about getting into coaching?" That was a high compliment coming from Coach Kincaid.

"Thanks, Coach. It seemed like the right call in the moment."

"Young man, that is the essence of coaching—analyzing where you are in the moment and making the best decision you can."

Coach Kincaid didn't say it, but I knew his theory could apply to anything in life. I couldn't turn back the hands of time, but I wished I could have embraced the coach's advice when I'd made a certain poor decision on the basketball court without first considering what would have been best in *that* moment.

"What are your plans beyond high school?" the coach asked me.

The coach always asked the good ones. The furthest ahead I was thinking was figuring out how we would get from Los

Angeles to the western regional three-on-three tournament in eastern Kansas on zero budget.

"I don't know, Coach." That was a true statement. I had no idea about my future. "I'd still like to play ball somewhere. I guess I've got to figure out what my options are."

Wade had a saying about options. He used to tell me that my options were as infinite as my ability to think them up. In the gym at that moment, all I could think about was going home to sleep.

"Tryouts here at Jefferson are in September," Coach Kincaid said. "Keep us in mind as an option if things don't work out for you elsewhere."

"Thanks, Coach. I will."

I had an option, which was one more than I'd had moments earlier.

"How'd you like the option of walking me home?"

The only thing better than Rebecca's hearing was her timing. My bike was parked outside, so that meant I would walk it home again. But this was not another walk of shame. This was a walk of possibilities.

"Sure."

I walked over to Curtis to check on his condition. "How's the wheel?"

"Just have to rest it for a couple of weeks," he said. "Gonna ACE, ice, and elevate at the beach, dude. See you Monday."

I bro-hugged Curtis and turned to find Stretch sitting on a bench deep in thought. "What's on your mind?" I asked.

"Trying to figure out where I'm going for lunch. Wanna join me?"

"I've got a higher calling," I said as I tilted my head in Rebecca's direction. "Maybe next time. Hey, I wonder if your dad will shave some time off your sentence when you show him the hardware."

Rebecca and I waved goodbye to the guys and exited the campus at Baylor Boulevard. We headed for our neighborhood, making our way in silence for several blocks before Rebecca elbowed me in the ribs. "What's on your mind?" she said.

I had been taking mental inventory of all the stuff I was trying to figure out. At the top of the list was Lawrence's prediction of the exodus of basketball from our world. In close second was this pretty girl I was escorting home. I had also zoned out thinking about Chip and how sometimes bad things happened to good people, and I wondered whether he would ever solve the mystery of the missing basketball gear. "Nothing, just basketball and stuff." I swung my focus back to Rebecca and decided the moment was right to ask her the question on my mind since the day we met. "How'd you end up at McDerney?"

Rebecca didn't say a word for three more blocks.

"Hello, anybody home?"

"Maybe next time," she said.

"That's what you said last time." I knew there had been fisticuffs involved, but I didn't say anything. Six more blocks went by. I decided to take the pressure off. "If you don't want to—"

"Punched an idiot jock in the face really hard, like, *really* hard."

Rebecca went back in time to explain that she had been a

junior at Gainesworth Prep, a private school in an upscale section of the city, enrolled in the sports medicine program, working with personnel who managed the medical needs of the football team. One afternoon after football practice, she was instructed to tape up the bruised ribs of the team's star quarterback.

"For some reason, he thought that entitled him to certain privileges," she said. "When I asked him to knock it off, he didn't stop, so I slugged him, like, as hard as I could. Kinda like when you belted that ref, only harder."

"Then what happened?"

"There was blood everywhere. I mean, *everywhere*. I think I broke his nose. Campus security shows up. Guy concocts a story, his teammates back him up, next thing I know, I'm at McDerney trying to figure out why Lawrence brings his lunch to school in a lead-lined suitcase."

A couple of weeks earlier, Rebecca had been this frustrating, tough, smart, and cute know-it-all stranger. She remained all of those things, but now . . . I'd never had a girlfriend before, so I could only imagine that this was what it must be like.

"Are you even listening to me, Ezekiel?"

Especially the frustrating part.

"Am I listening? I'm sure there's a perfectly reasonable explanation for Lawrence's lunchbox. I wonder if—"

Rebecca leaned in and kissed me on the cheek, releasing a swarm of butterflies in my stomach—the kind of feeling I might get if I ate a slice of pepperoni pizza while hitting a buzzer-beating thirty-footer.

"We finally got here," Rebecca said. I felt a wave of heat

track across my face as I turned beet red. "I meant, to my house," she said. "What were *you* thinking?"

I stammered something about how late it was getting, climbed onto my bike, and sailed all the way home. I ran up the building stairs, zipping past Mrs. Fenner before she could tell me to slow down, and walked through the front door of my apartment.

"Mom! We won!"

My mother was sitting at the kitchen table, the telephone pressed to her ear, hands trembling. There were tears in her eyes.

"Yes, sir, I understand," she said. "When can I expect to hear from you again?" Mom listened to a lengthy response before saying goodbye.

"What is it? What's wrong?"

My mother stood up and turned her focus to me. "You won? That's great, honey."

"What's going on? Who called?"

I knew it was something bad. She tried to answer but broke down and collapsed back into her chair. I waited for her to gather herself, my hand on her shoulder.

"That was a base commander from the Marine Corps Air Ground Combat Center Twentynine Palms."

I braced for the worst.

"Wade was shot while on a peacekeeping mission in Afghanistan."

"Is he alive?"

"He's alive, but he's in critical condition. They're trying to stabilize him so they can fly him to a military hospital in Germany for surgery."

Just like that, the best day of my life turned into the worst.

15

I Remembered My Heart Hurting

A military official called two days later to say that Wade's medical state had been upgraded from critical to serious, but he was not yet in a condition to fly.

I endured one more week of school and rode home Friday for the start of a weeklong spring break that would conclude with the western regional tournament at the University of Kansas.

Mrs. Fenner nabbed me as I carried my bike up the stairs. "What was that ruckus outside your apartment in the middle of the night last week?"

"Nothing, Mrs. Fenner, just some friends paying me a visit."

"I heard about what happened to Wade. Terrible thing. I hope he's going to be all right."

"Thank you, Mrs. Fenner. I'm sure everything will work out fine."

I walked into the apartment to a note from my mom saying that the Air Force had flown Wade from a marine base in Afghanistan to a medical center in Germany, the nearest treatment facility for U.S. soldiers wounded in Afghanistan. Wade would undergo surgery to repair several bullet wounds and remove shrapnel from his left leg. Mom's note also said she would be working the late shift at the hospital.

I focused on the more immediate crisis, the need to raise money for a Greyhound bus that would depart Los Angeles on Thursday night and arrive at the basketball arena Saturday morning, an hour before tipoff.

Curtis had searched the bottom of his sock drawer and under couch cushions for spare change. Stretch cut school to help his dad paint, but business was slow and he didn't make much. Their combined efforts netted all of twenty-five dollars—enough to buy a new basketball. This meant that, as unofficial team manager, I had to come up with the $1,000 we needed for bus tickets and food. There was no way I could ask my mom for that.

I made one final attempt to find my wayward ball. The last place I looked was my closet, where I found a cigar box that had belonged to my dad. When he moved out, he left it behind and Wade gave it to me for collecting stuff before he went into the marines.

Inside I found baseball cards, old coins, and the stack of envelopes I kept there. At the top of the stack was the letter my dad sent after he moved to Colorado. I remembered reading it and feeling upset afterward. Later when other letters arrived, I assumed they were more of the same, so I put them in the cigar box unopened.

I opened that first letter and read it again.

Dear Zeke,

This is a hard letter for me to write. By now you know I've moved out. I'm going to do the best I can to explain why. Your mother and I have not been happy together for a long time. It started when I returned home from serving in the Iraq War. I saw some terrible things happen to innocent people in that war. When I returned home, there was a lot of dark stuff going on inside my head. I was having nightmares and felt disconnected from the family, especially from your mother. It's important for you to understand this was not her fault or Wade's—or yours. In fact, you and Wade were the reason I stayed for as long as I did. When Wade left to join the corps, things between your mom and me got a lot worse. I felt trapped and isolated. I needed to run, so I worked out a transfer to the army's installation in Colorado. I thought it would be best for the future of our family for me to live apart from you.

I don't expect you to understand why I left. By no means am I saying it's okay for a father to walk away from his family. Leaving you behind was the hardest thing I've ever had to do. I knew your mother was strong enough to keep going. I knew you had close friends, especially Curtis and Stretch, who you trusted and who would look after you. That made it easier for me to justify my decision. It is

my sincerest hope that you will make better decisions in your life than I have in mine. I love you and always will.
Dad

I remembered my heart hurting when I read that letter for the first time. It was the reason why I had never opened any of the other envelopes. I pulled them out, five in total, seals intact. The postmarks were a year apart, around the time of my birthday. They bore the same Denver, Colorado, return address on the back flap.

I opened the first one and looked inside, not knowing what I would find. It was a birthday card with a short note written on it. When I pulled the card from the envelope, a rectangular piece of paper floated to the carpet. It was a personal check from my dad made out to Ezekiel Archer in the amount of $200. I opened the other four and found the same thing—more birthday cards and checks.

One thousand dollars had fallen out of the sky and landed on my closet floor.

16

I'm Sorry, There Are No Exceptions

I spent the weekend hanging out with Curtis and Stretch at the rec center preparing for the basketball competition that awaited us the following Saturday. The guys were relieved to find out about the birthday checks from my dad, which meant none of us would have to borrow money from our parents again.

Curtis's ankle had improved to the point where he could walk on it without wincing. Mr. Shields replaced the rims and nets that had disappeared from the center's basketball court, giving Curtis a chance to work on his outside shooting, but he had a long way to go before he could put much weight on his ankle.

Stretch made productive use of his time at the center with

numerous trips to the refrigerator, consuming enough food for ten men.

"Save room for dessert." That was Mr. Shields's diplomatic way of telling the Tall One to slow down.

"Don't worry," Stretch said, "I'm getting my second wind."

"What are you lads going to wear in Kansas?" Mr. Shields asked us. "Tournament rules mandate that all teams wear matching uniforms."

We'd barely figured out a way to travel to the tournament. Matching uniforms were beyond our reach.

Mr. Shields led us to a cardboard box resting against the back wall of the center's storage room. He pulled off the packing tape and took out a vintage basketball uniform—a hunter-green jersey with the number 30 stitched onto the front and back, and a pair of gold trunks with matching green piping. The style was at least a couple of decades old, but the fabric was still plush.

He handed it to Curtis. "That uniform was worn by the best shooter on our team, probably in all of Southern California," Mr. Shields said.

Mr. Shields then pulled out a uniform with the number 13 on it and gave it to Stretch. "You've got big shoes to fill. Our center wore this one, and he was first team all-state." Stretch's eyes grew as big as saucers as he inspected the garment.

Mr. Shields rummaged deeper. "Here you go," he said. It had a 23 on it, the number worn by Michael Jordan, one of my favorite players in the world. I was about to learn that a well-known local player had also worn that number.

"That jersey belonged to our point guard," Mr. Shields

said. "He was MVP of the state tournament. I think you know him as Coach Kincaid."

Mr. Shields explained that Jefferson Community College had worn these uniforms twenty-five years ago when the team won the California state championship. Mr. Shields was the head coach. Coach Kincaid was his starting point guard.

"How'd that box end up here?" I asked.

Mr. Shields said that when Coach Kincaid had taken over Jefferson's basketball program five years before and was settling into the coach's office, he found the box in the equipment room. "He called to ask whether the center would accept such a donation from the college, and I accepted. This will be the first time anyone has worn them since Jefferson won that title."

"I'm not so sure my dad's gonna like the jersey," Stretch said. "There's nothing on the back of it advertising his painting business."

"He'll get over it," Curtis said. "We appreciate the kind gesture, Mr. Shields."

I thanked Mr. Shields for looking after us, and the guys and I went our separate ways home.

Mom and I waited the rest of the weekend for another call from the marines, which came Sunday night. The military official said Wade had made it through surgery and was in serious condition but resting comfortably. It was the best news we could hope for.

Monday was the first day of spring break, ordinarily a time for playing basketball and goofing off with my friends. But with the bus trip three days away, there was much to do.

I showered and got dressed in preparation for a bike ride to Pacific Community Savings, the bank on which my dad's checks were drawn.

"What can I help you with, young man?" The woman at the teller window wore a lot of makeup and had a nametag that read: ELAINE STALLWORTH. She smiled and seemed friendly enough, so my nervousness faded. I reached into my jacket pocket. "I'm here to cash these five checks from my dad." I thought the direct approach was best.

Ms. Stallworth inspected the checks, reading each one carefully and even holding them up to the light to search for who-knows-what. Then she punched some numbers and letters into her keyboard before staring long and hard at her computer screen.

"Can I see some ID?" she said.

Stretch told me to be ready for that one. "Sure thing. Here's my library card."

Ms. Stallworth responded with words of discouragement, delivering them with a steely-eyed smirk-smile. "I'm afraid you're going to need more than your library card, young man."

When Ms. Stallworth "young-manned" me for a second time, I didn't take it as a good sign. I summoned my inner Stretch and went for broke. "See here, Ms. Stallworth. The library doesn't seem to have a problem with that card. I'm not sure why the bank would."

The blood drained from Ms. Stallworth's face before it rushed back in with full force. "Wait here. I'll be right back."

She gathered up my library card and my checks and

walked off to find the police, or maybe the bank manager. I felt a chilly bead of sweat roll across my forehead. If the bank wouldn't cash my checks, we could kiss the western regional tournament goodbye. I would have stood there spinning a basketball if I still owned one.

A few minutes later, Ms. Stallworth returned with a middle-aged man wearing a dark suit, neatly pressed shirt, and matching tie. "I'm Lyle Lester, the bank manager. I understand you'd like to cash these checks."

"Yes, sir."

"Do you have an additional form of identification?"

"Sir?"

"Do you have a driver's license?" Lyle Lester was friendly but persistent.

"No, sir, I don't drive."

"Do you have any other type of ID?"

I reached into my back pocket for my wallet and thumbed through everything in there until I found my McDerney student ID and a rec center membership card with my name on it but no photo. I offered them to the bank manager.

"I'm sorry, Ezekiel, but the bank won't be able to cash the checks without proper identification," Lyle Lester said. "One thousand dollars is a great deal of money, and this institution has its rules."

I had one more play left in me. If it had worked on Coach Kincaid, it was worth a shot with the bank manager. "Do you think you could make an exception in this case?"

There wasn't enough time to feel disappointed because the reply from Lyle Lester arrived too swiftly.

"I'm sorry, there are no exceptions at Pacific Community Savings. Good day, Ezekiel."

Not really. It wasn't a good day at all. We had no money and no hope of boarding the Kansas-bound Greyhound bus on Thursday.

Stick a fork in Curtis, Stretch, and me. We were done.

17

We Interrupt This Program to Bring You a Special News Bulletin

I put everything back in my wallet and headed for the exit. I couldn't decide if I would ride to Curtis's house first or Stretch's place to deliver the bad news. On one hand, Curtis would be relieved to know he wouldn't have to test his sprained ankle anytime soon. On the other hand, Stretch would overreact and throw a fit before calming himself down with a club sandwich and a box of cookies. Or I could ride over to Rebecca's house. She would listen and empathize with me.

"Excuse me, Ezekiel." The bank manager scooted across the lobby to catch me before I reached the door. "You don't by any chance have a brother named Wade Archer, do you?"

That was a question I wasn't expecting. "Yes, Wade's my brother."

"Come with me." Mr. Lester took me back to Ms. Stallworth's teller window. There was already another bank customer in mid-transaction, but Lyle Lester whisked that person to another window and returned.

"Your brother is in the Marine Corps, right?"

"Yes, sir."

"I recognized the resemblance. I've seen a picture of him."

"Sir?"

"When my youngest son enlisted in the Marine Corps, he called to tell me he was having a tough go of it early on in boot camp. Then he sent me a letter a month into basic training saying that one of the other recruits was looking after him. It was your brother." Lyle Lester pulled a wallet from his suit jacket and showed me a photograph of his son alongside Wade and other marines at an outdoor basketball court on the base.

Lyle Lester instructed Ms. Stallworth to cash my checks.

"Only one of them was written in the previous twelve months," Ms. Stallworth said. "The other four are older and fall outside of bank policy."

"That's all right, Elaine," Lyle Lester said. "We can make an exception and cash all five of them. It's my way of saying thanks." Then he asked me a question I had no idea how to answer. "How is Wade anyway?"

I wished I knew. "He's fine. I'll tell him you said hello." I put the ten crisp hundred-dollar bills into my wallet and rode home.

It was Thursday before we knew it. The guys and I packed our duffel bags and were ready to hit the road. The Greyhound bus was scheduled to depart from downtown Los Angeles at 6:45 p.m. Stretch's dad would drive us to the bus station in his Puckett Painting van, so all we had to do was show up on time and buy our tickets.

I had enough time to get a new basketball before the trip. Chip's Sporting Goods had had its grand reopening the day before, so I went there instead of Global Mega-Sports.

"I suppose you're here to pick up a new ball for the big trip to Kansas," Chip said. "Check out our new basketball section."

He had a ton of new equipment in stock. I selected a durable indoor-outdoor ball, gave it a quick fingertip spin, and met Chip at the cash register. He rang it up and I handed him a hundred-dollar bill.

"Rob a bank?"

I thought about the irony of Chip's words. I admired how he stayed on an even keel all the time, no matter what happened at his store. He wished me luck in the tournament, and I headed for home to wait for Puckett Shuttle Service to pick me up.

Remember when I said that strange things had started happening right after I enrolled in McDerney a few weeks earlier? What happened next was an eleven out of ten on the weirdness scale.

I had my new ball tucked under my arm as I pedaled down Drexler Drive for home. Out of the corner of my eye, I caught a glimpse of a bright, fiery object in the sky streaking diagonally toward Earth at tremendous speed. It appeared to crash into Chip's Sporting Goods. The thunderous explosion scrambled my eardrums. I didn't know whether it was a missile or a meteorite or worse.

The shockwave from the blast knocked me off my bike. My bare hands scraped the ground as I tried to break my fall. I must have hit my head on the asphalt, because I blacked out. The sound of police cars and fire trucks screaming down the street brought me back to reality.

My hands were stinging, and I looked down to see that they were covered in dirt and blood. I wanted to follow the authorities and see what had happened, but I felt groggy from the fall, and it was too close to the Greyhound's departure time, so I pedaled the rest of the way home.

I scrambled up the stairs to my apartment and ran cold water from the kitchen faucet over my hands to ease the sting from my fall. I noticed a note from my mom on the countertop:

Hi, honey,

The military official said your brother is alert and restless. That's hardly news to those of us who know him. Please keep a good thought.

Love,

Mom

No problem there. Wade was always in my thoughts.

I turned my attention to finding out what had caused the explosion. I went into my closet and pulled out an old AM radio that had once belonged to my dad. I plugged it in, clicked it on, and spun the dial to the all-news station.

Then I heard it:

"We interrupt this program to bring you a special news bulletin. A meteorite has crashed into Chip's Sporting Goods on Drexler Drive. The LAPD is reporting no fatalities and one person injured inside. Damage appears to be confined to the store's new basketball section. We will bring you further bulletins as this story develops. We now return to our regularly scheduled programming."

I turned off the radio and collapsed onto my bedroom floor. Everything was piling on top of me, making it hard to breathe. First the fight, then the forfeit, the expulsion, and the loss of my scholarship. Then Wade is wounded on, of all things, a peacekeeping mission. Then a meteorite takes out Chip's, and the nerdy autistic kid will no doubt think I caused it.

My chest tightened. My fingers tingled, and it wasn't a good kind of tingling, like when you catch a hard chest pass solidly or feel the ball peeling off your palm for a layup. My mouth filled with cotton as my body went cold and damp. I was losing the battle to pull air into my lungs. I was freefalling into a bottomless pit. There was nothing I could grab onto to make it stop.

18

It Was Time to Terminate the Experiment

My stomach rumbled in protest over what was going on in the rest of my body. I crawled to the bathroom. What happened next was something Stretch would refer to as re-carpeting the igloo or making copies of the menu. Curtis was too much of a gentleman to choose such tacky ways to describe it.

I arrived just in time—and I'll say this as diplomatically as possible—to pray at the porcelain altar. I wondered whether Mrs. Fenner could hear me barfing from across the hall. If she could, would she think someone was trying to fold me in half?

I filled my lungs with the deepest breath of air I have ever taken. It cleared my head of everything but one question: Was it possible that what Lawrence was telling me was—*for real*?

There was only one way to find out. I had to confront him, and I had to do it right now.

I checked my watch: five o'clock. Stretch's dad would be at my apartment at six-fifteen. That meant I had one hour to unravel the greatest basketball mystery of our generation and make it home to catch a ride.

Wade used to tell me to always be prepared, so I put my new basketball in my duffel bag and threw it over my shoulder for the ride to Lawrence's house, just in case.

"What was all that—"

"Not now, Mrs. Fenner!" I said as I flew down the stairs and pedaled away at warp speed. I knew where Lawrence lived from when I'd walked him home a few weeks back. It was three miles away, so I had to hustle.

I propped my bike against a sycamore tree on Lawrence's front lawn. My lungs burned as they begged for oxygen. I bent over to catch my breath. The bus ride would be my best chance to rest before the western regional tournament. I looked forward to closing my eyes and drifting off once I could convince Lawrence to come clean.

I knocked on the front door. No answer. I knocked again, harder this time. My mind drifted to something Lawrence had written a few weeks before about basketball ceasing to exist on the third Friday in April. I did some calendar math in my head—that was the next day. I knocked even harder and the door swung open.

"Hello, there. Are you lost?"

I was lost, but not in the way Lawrence's father thought I was.

"Is Lawrence home? I'm Zeke, a friend of his. I really need to speak with him."

Lawrence's dad was surprised to learn his son had a visitor and amused for a reason I was about to find out. "Oh, you mean Sherman."

Was this the right house? "Sir?"

"Lawrence is sort of a nickname. Ever since Sherman learned to speak, he's been mesmerized by that city, completely fixated on it."

"What city?"

"Lawrence."

"Sir?"

"Lawrence, Kansas. You know, home of the University of Kansas."

No, I didn't know. I figured the university was someplace in Kansas where it belonged. I had no idea what to make of this new development.

"Sherman, you've got company." Lawrence's dad pointed toward his son's bedroom. "Down the hall on the left. He's in there doing math homework." I dropped my duffel bag and went down the hallway. "He doesn't talk much, but he talks about you all the time. Says you look after him at school. I appreciate that."

"Yes, sir."

I knocked on Lawrence's door. "It's Zeke. I need to speak with you."

"Go away."

"Lawrence, I don't have a lot of time. Open the door."

"Go away. It's too late."

I turned the doorknob and let myself in. The first thing I noticed was a wall clock that read 5:17. Lawrence was at his desk, a book on quantum physics open in front of him.

"Guess you heard what happened at Chip's Sporting Goods this afternoon," I said. "The news media is claiming a meteorite crashed into the store and took out all of Chip's basketball gear. Sounds kinda weird, don't you think? Know anything about that?"

Lawrence didn't say anything and didn't look up.

"I'm talking to you! I need you to tell me what's going on."

Lawrence turned the page and kept reading. He had either gone selectively deaf since the last time we spoke, or he was flat-out ignoring me.

"We're supposed to be friends," I said.

"They're taking the game away," Lawrence said. His face reddened. I thought I felt a wave of heat coming from his direction. "Now you know. Guess you can leave."

"I'm not leaving until you tell me everything." That wasn't necessarily true, because I needed to get home in a matter of minutes to catch a ride to the bus terminal. "If all this basketball-going-away stuff is really my fault like you say it is, then you have an obligation to tell me why—*please*."

I figured the number of times anyone had ever sincerely said *please* to Lawrence could be counted on one hand, with change.

"The 7th Dimension," he said.

A journey of a thousand miles begins with a single step.

"Perhaps you can start at the beginning."

Lawrence laid his book on the bed, reached for his pad, and pulled a pencil from his pocket protector. After protecting the secret for so long, he let his guard down all at once and began writing furiously. Granted, Lawrence was only an underage high school junior, but that was a long time to hold on to something so important for so long. He rocked back and forth in his chair, never once looking up. When he had finished writing, he ripped the piece of paper from the pad, folded it in half, and held it out. I had no idea what he was about to tell me.

> *The 7th Dimension. Inter-dimensional Entity. Lives in the interconnected root system of trees around the world.*

I buckled my mental seatbelt. I had a feeling I was in for a rough ride.

> *The 7th Dimension's secret emissary was James Naismith, little-known Canadian physical educator, medical doctor, and minister. Working through Dr. Naismith, the Entity brought basketball to humankind in the winter of 1891 as a means of fostering peace and brotherhood on Earth.*

In junior high, I had written a term paper on the history of basketball. I learned about Dr. Naismith from a biography I found at the library. He was the game's inventor and an honorable man. He was resourceful, too, using peach baskets as the first basketball goals.

> *7th Dimension world headquarters are within the intertwined roots of a grove of oak, sycamore, and pine trees living adjacent to Allen Fieldhouse, indoor arena on the campus of the University of Kansas, city of Lawrence. The university is considered the birthplace of basketball.*

That was an eyeful, but it still wasn't making any sense.

> *My father is an architect. There were always pencils and drafting tools around the house. When I was four, I used the ancient Greek geometric technique of neusis construction to develop a triangle on a piece of paper using a compass and a marked straightedge. With those same tools, I circumscribed a heptagon around the triangle, then laid out seven precisely measured and beveled No. 2 pencils over the heptagonal figure to create the exact seven-sided antenna needed to intercept Entity communiqués.*

Of course he had. Lawrence's note went on to explain that when he had first told me about the 7th Dimension's decision, it warned him never to mention it again.

> *Entity modified its spectral subcarrier, thinking that would stop me from eavesdropping, but I formulated a workaround. It miffed the Entity.*

I still didn't understand what all of that had to do with me. I kept reading:

> *The game accomplished its intended purpose for decades. But when humanity strayed from the path through violence, greed, and corruption, the Entity concluded it was time to terminate the experiment. The breaking point occurred at the city finals, when you punched out a referee.*

The next thing Lawrence wrote sent a cold chill down my spine:

> *Basketball will cease to exist tomorrow at midnight. They say there's nothing anyone can do to stop it.*

Ballgame.

19

I Need Your Dad's Bolt Cutters

Let me see if I had this straight: Lawrence had used a seven-sided crystal radio on steroids to monitor the rise and fall of basketball around the globe, then concluded it would all go up in smoke because I'd tried to slug Brock Decker—and missed.

That was the CliffsNotes version of the predicament I was in. It had to be pure fantasy. No way any of it could be true. Lawrence had finally gone bonkers.

"You're kidding, right?"

"No."

"How can I stop it from happening?"

"Can't."

"Look me in the eye and tell me what you're saying is true."

Lawrence didn't, or couldn't, look me in the eye, but he complied with the other half of my demand. "It's true."

I had two choices: I could either take a bus to Kansas and arrive on Saturday morning for a tournament Lawrence said wouldn't happen, or I could try to get there by the midnight Friday deadline and convince the 7th Dimension to make an exception.

I considered flipping a coin to decide. That way, if it were the wrong decision, at least I could blame the coin.

As berserk as this 7th Dimension business sounded, my gut instinct was to take Lawrence at his word, because if he were right, at least I'd know I had done everything I could to save the game.

So I gave in.

"Okay, you win."

I took the leap of faith without knowing where it would lead or the dangers I would face. The room began to spin and my legs wobbled as I lost my balance and stumbled backward. I felt a sharp jolt against my upper back as Lawrence's bedroom wall caught my fall.

I cleared the fog from my head and did a reality check. It was Thursday. The bus would leave in a little over an hour, at 6:45 p.m., and wouldn't arrive at the University of Kansas until Saturday morning at 8:55 for a tournament that would start about an hour later, at 10:00. Since the 7th Dimension was going to pull the plug on Friday at midnight, it meant the bus wouldn't make it on time. I had to find another way to get there.

Lawrence removed the seven pencils from his pocket protector and interconnected them on his desk in a heptagonal configuration. He tilted his head at a forty-five-degree angle and closed his eyes. I watched as his body vibrated and then went limp. When he came to, he picked up his pad and wrote even more furiously than before. He tore the paper from his pad, folded it, and offered it to me:

> KU is 1,580 miles from here. We'll need a car.

Thanks, Lawrence. Really helpful, buddy. I kept reading:

> If we leave at 6:45 p.m. and drive at 65 mph, assuming a conservative 200 miles per tank of gas and stopping for gas 8 times at 5 minutes per stop, taking into account weather conditions, altitude, road topography, and the loss of 2 hours as we travel across 2 time zones, we will arrive at the University of Kansas on Friday night at precisely 8:38 p.m. Central Daylight Time.

That itinerary would leave plenty of time for a face-to-face chinwag with 7th Dimension honchos. It was a cinch. All I had to do was show up at the clandestine-grove help desk and ask for the life force in charge.

Hey, wait a second. If *we* leave at 6:45? We? And how in the world were *we* going to drive there? I had no driver's license and no vehicle. After Wade had shipped out with the marines, my mom had grown very worried about my safety. She just didn't want me to drive. She could drive me wherever my bike couldn't take me, she promised. So, to put her mind at ease, I had just kept postponing getting my license.

"I don't know how I'm going to get there, but I know you can't come with me."

"You need me."

"I can't take you along." I had gotten the world into this mess. I had to make it right all by myself. I threw everything at Lawrence I could think of to make him understand. "It's too risky. Your dad won't let you go. You have homework." Then I tossed in the kitchen sink for the closer: "I don't need a mathematician on this trip."

"Can't do it without me."

Maybe he was right. Then again, maybe Rebecca was right. I could hear her voice in my head: *"You're Ezekiel Archer. You can do anything you set your mind to."*

I could do it, but I couldn't take the kid along. That was that.

"I'm sorry, Lawrence, I have to leave now."

I went for the door but stopped dead in my tracks. There was one small detail I had failed to consider. How was I going to plead my case to the 7th Dimension if Lawrence was the only person who was able to communicate with it?

"Lawrence, how do I—"

Lawrence had anticipated the question. He gathered the pencils from his desk and handed them to me. The pencils were freshly beveled, the points sharpened and aimed upward.

"You'll need these."

I put the pencils in the back pocket of my jeans. "Thanks. I owe you one."

Lawrence rocked from side to side in his chair and didn't say another word. I waved goodbye to his dad as I picked up my duffel bag and rode away as fast as I could. I got a few blocks down the street before pulling to the curb. I straddled my bike frame, trying to catch my breath as I took stock of my dilemma. I had no idea where I was pedaling, but I needed a car to get to eastern Kansas in the next twenty-four hours. Even if I had one, I wouldn't know how to drive it.

Then it happened.

Mr. Shields equated it to five teammates on a basketball court whose names were Comprehension, Recognition, Insight, Inspiration, and Sudden Realization. It was a formidable team known as the Aha Moment.

I got an idea. Or rather an idea hit me.

I raced for Stretch's house, dodging cars and riding through stop signs all the way there.

"I thought we were going to pick you up," Stretch said, standing in his doorway, a look of confusion contorting his long face.

"I need your dad's bolt cutters."

"Why?"

"No time to explain. Just get them. I promise I'll bring them back."

Stretch opened the garage door and took the bolt cutters from his dad's van. I wedged the tool into my duffel bag and handed Stretch $600 from my wallet.

"Here."

"No, you can just borrow them. My dad won't mind."

It was hard to tell if Stretch was working me or was genuinely confused.

"It's for bus tickets for you and Curtis."

"What are you talking about? My dad's taking us to the bus station in a few minutes. You can pay for our tickets when we get there."

I'd promised Lawrence I wouldn't tell anyone about the 7th Dimension. I knew I couldn't violate that trust, not even with Stretch, one of my best friends in the world. "Take it," I said. "I can't ride the bus, and I can't explain why. I'll see you guys Saturday at the tournament. Tell my mom I'm okay."

"You're not making any sense."

Nothing was making sense, and what I was about to do wasn't going to help.

I sailed down Russell Road until I reached the entrance to Biffmann Self-Storage. The owner, Chett Biffmann, was sitting at the front desk. The pungent aroma of chewing tobacco invaded my nostrils as I walked in.

Chett Biffmann was a portly man who had as many chins as he had consonants in his last name. He was nosy and talkative, with a gray beard and a thick Southern drawl. He ran a tight ship, and anyone in town with important extra stuff to store always stored it at Biffmann Self-Storage.

"I need to get into space 1046."

"Say, you're that fella who's always walking around with that darned basketball in his hands. Zeke, right?"

"Yes, sir, that's me. Can you tell me where I can find space 1046?"

"Well I'll be gasted in the flabber regions. You're Wade's brother, aren't you?" Chett Biffmann said. "I heard he joined the Marine Corps. How's he doing, anyhow?"

"He's good. I don't mean to be rude, sir, but I really need to get into space 1046."

"Tarnation, son, you must have ants in your pants. Through that door, make a right, last row in the back. You'll need the key to open the padlock."

I had that part covered. "Yeah, thanks. I'll tell Wade you said hi."

I rode through the aisles all the way to the last row, shuttling past dozens of corrugated metal storage units until I came to space 1046. My duffel bag thumped as it hit the ground. I took a look around. The coast was clear.

Snap!

Mr. Puckett's bolt cutters sliced through Wade's padlock like a Curtis Short fade-away jumper dancing across the steel chain basketball nets at the rec center.

I took hold of the roll-up door's steel handle and opened it. The faint taste of gasoline raked across my throat as I flipped on the light switch. There it was, protected by a black tarp, just the way Wade had left it five years before when he took off for boot camp.

Dust scattered into the dank air as I pulled off the tarp. The vehicle's sea-foam-green paint glistened under a lone incandescent light bulb.

It was Wade's 1965 Chevrolet Shortbed Fleetside pickup truck.

I rubbed my hands down my pant legs trying to remove

the sweat, but it didn't help. No way could this be a good idea. Wade would either kill me or tell Mom first and then kill me.

Wade and my father had bought the pickup truck from an old army buddy of Dad's. The truck was broken down at the time, and the body and upholstery were in terrible shape. Wade and Dad spent the next two years working on it in the carport behind our apartment building. Dad set up a makeshift backboard on the side of the building so I could hang out and shoot around while they rebuilt the 283-cubic-inch V8 engine, restored the truck's interior, and repainted the body in its original color.

Wade used to drive me to basketball practice in that truck. I was mesmerized by how fluidly he operated the three-on-the-tree gearshift mounted on the steering column. "Knee, elbow, wrist," he used to tell me as he stepped on the clutch while easing the shifter into the next gear. Wade knew that the best way to get through to me was with the language of basketball, so he showed me how to operate the truck's transmission by referencing the proper way to shoot a free throw. I was twelve years old at the time.

Wade taught me how to *really* drive a stick on the sly just before putting his prized pickup truck into storage when he left for boot camp. I never had a chance to practice after that, and this was the first time the Chevy had seen the light of day since then.

I hoisted my bike and duffel bag into the truck bed. The door squeaked on its hinges as I pulled it open and stepped inside. The springy leather-upholstered seat felt familiar against my backside. I tugged at the sun visor, and a set of car keys jangled onto my lap.

It was the only way I could get to the University of Kansas in time to save basketball from extinction. I moved the bench seat forward, adjusted the mirrors, and fastened my seatbelt. I eased the key into the ignition switch, stepped on the clutch, and turned the key.

Nothing.

I tried again, but the only noise I heard was my heart beating against my chest.

If there were a scoreboard mounted on the dashboard, it would have read:

7th DIMENSION	*ZEKE*
1	*0*

20

Was It Kidnapping If the Weird Kid Actually Wanted to Go?

The battery was dead. I might as well have been too.

It wasn't realistic to think Wade's antique pickup truck could make it all the way to eastern Kansas, so I reasoned it was for the best that it didn't start, since I wouldn't remember how to drive it anyway.

On an impulse that must've come from my heart, not my head, I glanced at my watch, hoping time had stood still. Nope, it was seven o'clock straight up. The Greyhound bus had left the station fifteen minutes earlier. That meant I had no chance of playing in a basketball tournament that wouldn't happen anyway. Not even a miracle could get me out of the hammerlock I'd gotten myself into.

"Need a jump?"

The angel of mercy wore soiled work boots and a massive pair of tobacco-juice-stained overalls. It was Chett Biffmann, riding up in the Biffmann Self-Storage golf cart with a car battery custom mounted onto the rear bumper.

"Figured that old thang wouldn't start. Pop the hood for me, son."

I knew how to release the hood latch after watching Wade and my dad do it so many times. I raised the Chevy's hood, and Chett clamped a set of jumper cables onto Wade's battery.

"Give her a try."

I pushed down on the clutch, pumped the gas pedal, and turned the key.

Tucka-thuck, tucka-thuck, tucka-thuck, tucka-thuck, tucka-thuck, tucka-thuck, tucka-thuck—vroooooooom!

The engine coughed and roared to life.

"That's what she sounded like when Wade backed her in there a while back. Must be the proper storage conditions," Chett said, slapping himself so hard on the thigh that my own thigh stung. He roared in laughter, his ample chins jiggling as he unclipped the jumper cables. "Ease her on outta there, son."

The only reason I knew how to start it was because I'd watched how Wade turned the engine over whenever he took me for a ride. Actually driving it, however, was another matter.

Chett hawked a wad of tobacco juice that splashed onto the asphalt as I jerked my foot off the clutch, lurching the truck forward. That was immediately followed by what sounded like a mule kicking the underside of the hood as the engine died and my forehead banged against the steering wheel.

Chett laughed even harder than before as he reconnected the jumpers. "Easy does it, son. You gotta treat her like a lady, nice and gentle-like."

I pondered Chett's unsolicited perspective on relationship etiquette when I remembered the time Wade taught me how to find the gearshift's friction point. Wade described it as the moment when releasing the clutch and giving it gas caused the truck to move. I turned the key a second time.

Tucka-thuck, tucka-thuck—vroooooooom!

Chett Biffmann released the cables as I revved the engine a couple of times. I maneuvered the two floor pedals in opposite directions and slowly pulled the truck out of the storage unit, braking to a stop under the dusky twilight sky.

"Wade know you're taking her out for a spin?"

I moved my shift hand behind my back and crossed my fingers, hoping it would soften the lie I was about to tell Chett Biffmann.

"Yes, sir. He asked me to make sure everything was working okay. I'll have it back in a jiffy."

Chett waved goodbye and lowered the metal door as I exited Biffmann Self-Storage, heading east on Russell Road. The street took me in the direction of my neighborhood, so I cruised over to Rebecca's house to let her know I was taking Wade's truck to Kansas and would be back home in a few days.

I left the engine running as I knocked on Rebecca's door. She opened it just wide enough to peek her head around.

"Hey, so, I'm, like, taking off for Kansas, and I wanted to, you know, stop by and, like, say hello and goodbye and stuff."

"Not a good time for me."

Not exactly the reception I had hoped for. Rebecca stepped back to close the door, but a hand came forward and swung it open.

"Real smooth, dweeb. You practice that all the way here?"

I was used to Brock Decker coming between me and everything important in my life. Now he was with Rebecca, my almost-sort-of girlfriend, and they were in *her house*. I was too stunned to speak. This couldn't be happening. My stomach clenched as I lumbered back to Wade's truck.

"Ezekiel, wait, I can explain."

Not interested. I flung my body into the driver's seat.

Crunch!

I reached into my back pocket to pull out Lawrence's pencils, only to find I'd snapped all of them in half. I slammed the truck's door, popped the clutch, and burned rubber into the darkness. The tears in my eyes didn't dry until I was twenty miles outside Barstow on Interstate 15. I was driving a decades-old stolen pickup truck down a crowded interstate to a destination I had no idea how to find. Even if I found 7th Dimension headquarters, it wouldn't matter, because I had destroyed my only means of communicating with the otherworldly Entity that had the power to make everything okay again.

As if all that weren't enough, the gas tank was empty.

Bam! Bam! Bam!

It sounded like I had run over a deer. I felt my heart pound out a paradiddle in my chest cavity: *THUMP-a-thump-thump, THUMP-a-thump-thump . . .*

Bam! Bam! Bam!

It had happened again, harder. I looked in the rearview

mirror and saw the shadowy outline of a horrible creature in the truck bed. I panicked and swerved to the right, nearly losing control as I crossed two lanes of traffic and veered directly into the path of an eighteen-wheeler. The big-rig driver laid on his horn. The shrill sound clanged through my skull as I steered away from a fiery death and locked up the wheels, skidding to a stop on the shoulder of the highway.

Dust swirled in all directions. I took another look in the rearview mirror. Nothing there. Was I seeing things? I tiptoed into the dark night and clenched a fist, ready for anything that could come at me. I moved to the side of the truck and peered over the metal panel. My bike and duffel bag were right where I'd left them, but what was that metal box, and what was wiggling around in the truck bed behind it?

The creature raised its head.

It was Lawrence.

"What are you doing here!" I shouted. "You scared the crap out of me!" No response, which was what I'd come to expect from attempting a conversation with Lawrence. "Are you nuts? I said you couldn't come with me. Does your dad know where you are? You have to leave right now. It's kidnapping. I could go to jail."

I wondered whether the cops would think it was kidnapping if the weird kid actually wanted to go. I lowered the tailgate. Lawrence grabbed onto the handle of his metal lunchbox and hopped onto the gravelly pavement below.

Then without uttering a word, he turned and began walking back toward Los Angeles.

21

Want Some Gum?

I watched in disbelief as Lawrence put one foot in front of the other along the shoulder of Interstate 15 in the opposite direction of traffic, cars whizzing past him a few feet away. If he kept a brisk pace and didn't detour for too long at the rest stops dotting the highway, he might make it home—never. Good grief.

"*Lawrence!*"

No doubt he was interested in making good time, because he never turned around. I pulled the car keys from the ignition and jogged after him, my sneakers crunching on the stones and debris on the side of the road. Even when I caught up to him, he didn't stop. Pure focus. There was beauty in that. I stepped in front of him to block his path. Lawrence finally stopped.

"Okay, you win. I guess we're going to Kansas."

Lawrence pivoted on his heel and walked back to the truck. He dropped his metal lunchbox onto the floorboard of the cab and climbed in as I started the engine and pulled back onto the highway.

"We need gas. We're on empty."

"Exit on East Main Street, one-point-seven miles ahead."

"How do you know that?" I asked, knowing full well he wouldn't answer me, which was sort of an answer in itself. I was getting better at interpreting Lawrence's non-replies. It was like figuring out the opposing team's defensive strategy, only without the advantage of having teammates, a court, and a basketball.

We exited the highway exactly 1.7 miles later in Barstow and pulled into a gas station. I eased the pickup next to a gas pump and cut the ignition, then pulled a dollar out of my wallet.

"Use this to call your dad. Tell him you're with me and we'll be back in a couple of days."

Lawrence took the dollar inside the service station's mini-market while I handed a hundred-dollar bill to the cashier. I squeezed as much gas into the Chevy as it would hold, went back for my change, and waited inside the truck. When Lawrence came out, we drove back onto the interstate heading east.

"What did he say?" I asked.

"Who?"

It wasn't much of an answer, but at least he had given me one. "Your dad. What did he say when you told him?"

"Want some gum?"

"He asked if you wanted some gum?"

No reply. Lawrence was agitated. He opened his metal lunchbox and pulled out the same pad of paper he had used to write on in his bedroom. He took a pencil from his pocket protector—yes, he had restocked his supply—and wrote as furiously as ever. When he finished, he tore out the piece of paper, folded it in half, and held it out for me.

"Can't read that. I'm driving. It's too dark."

Lawrence folded the note a few more times and stuffed it into his shirt pocket behind the pocket protector.

"I've got an idea," I said. "Why don't you read it to me."

Lawrence unfolded the piece of paper. "Dad always says to chew bubble gum when I'm nervous."

There was another long pause. "Go on."

"Didn't have any. Used the dollar to buy a pack. Want some?"

I knew right then that I would go to jail, no question about it. "Sure, I'll take a piece."

There we were, two eastbound, gum-chewing amigos on a road trip into the unknown. Lawrence calmed down, taking comfort in an ample wad of bubble gum. I measured our progress by the sound of Lawrence snapping a bubble whenever we passed a mile marker. As navigators go, he was thorough and consistent.

Not a word was spoken between us as we drove for a couple more hours while Lawrence kept a steady beat of popping bubbles. Midnight was approaching when I felt the call of nature. "I've got to use the bathroom. You need to call your dad. Where's the next town?"

"Vegas, baby."

Apparently, Lawrence spent time watching TV in between

homework assignments. Sure enough, just as we hit the peak summit of a mountain range and began our descent into the valley below, there they were: the bright lights of Sin City.

We exited the highway and I guided the truck into a parking space at World Famous Calvin's Gas, Food & Casino. World Famous Calvin's had everything the weary traveler could want, all under one sun-parched roof.

As we walked inside, I pulled out my wallet to take inventory. Minus the $600 I'd given Stretch for bus tickets, subtracting the basketball I'd bought at Chip's Sporting Goods, and factoring in the dollar I'd given Lawrence in Barstow plus the gas we bought there, I had about $350 to get us all the way to eastern Kansas.

I peeled off a five-dollar bill and gave Lawrence specific instructions: "Get yourself something to eat and go call your dad." Lawrence didn't respond, but he took the money and went over to the food aisle. I headed for the cashier's window to ask the store clerk where the restroom was.

"You can't use it unless you have the key," said the clerk, who had the word CALVIN embroidered on his shirt. I didn't know if he was the real Calvin, or a guy working there whose name happened also to be Calvin, or some random clerk who had forgotten his shirt and borrowed it from one of the two aforementioned Calvins.

"How do I get the key?"

"You can't, unless you buy something."

"I've got a friend in there buying something right now."

"That only counts if *he* needs to use the restroom. You still won't get the key," Calvin said.

Good grief. I snatched a pack of bubble gum from the candy display and bounced it off the counter.

"That'll be one dollar."

I handed Calvin a dollar bill and slid the bubble gum into my pocket. "Can I get that key now?"

"Someone already has it. You'll have to wait in that line over there."

Calvin pointed toward the restroom door. The line was six guys deep. As I took my place at the back of the queue, I wondered whether World Famous Calvin's Gas, Food & Casino used the restroom-key ploy to sell more bubble gum. I looked around for Lawrence. No sign of him. Another twenty minutes passed before it was my turn to go in.

When I came out, I handed the key to the next guy in line and walked outside to gas up the truck. I went back in to search the food store for Lawrence, but he was nowhere to be found. My instincts told me he had wandered into the casino, and that's when things got a lot weirder.

The cigarette smoke hanging in the casino air was so thick that it made my eyes sting. I scanned the casino through the haze and spotted Lawrence parked in front of—and I'm not making this up—a basketball-themed slot machine. He dropped a coin into the slot, pulled the handle, and released it. I watched as the wheels spun around before locking into place.

Thunk! Thunk! Thunk!

Sevens, three of them, all in a row.

Lawrence had hit the jackpot.

A blaring horn pummeled my eardrums, followed by the sound of a bell ringing that was reminiscent of being late for fifth period at McDerney. An old geezer in a cowboy hat gambling at a nearby slot machine moseyed over and slapped Lawrence really hard on the back.

"Way to go, podner," the geezer said. "You just broke the bank!"

Lawrence stared up at the slot machine's numerical display, which was blinking $7,777,777 in red lights. He was rich, all right, but there was one catch—he was only fourteen years old.

From the corner of my eye, I caught a glimpse of a security guard walking toward us. Right behind him was a rotund, balding man carrying a clipboard. Maybe it was the real Calvin, or the FBI, or the 7th Dimension's casino field representative.

"Congratulations, fellas," said the man with the clipboard.

Lawrence turned and walked toward the exit. But instead of his moving with his usual gait, he was race-walking—that sport where you walk really fast, and one foot must remain in contact with the ground at all times. He race-walked right out the front door without ever turning around.

22

Tastes Like Chicken

We got to the pickup truck as the possible real Calvin came outside, huffing and puffing as he waved in vain with his clipboard. I couldn't make out exactly what he said over the roar of the engine as I started the truck, but I thought it was something like, "Hey, wait! Your money!"

I burned rubber in first gear all the way to the freeway on-ramp as the foul smell of tire smoke came up through the floorboards and filled the truck's cabin. I cranked down my window with my left hand, shifted into second gear with my right, and floored it, sending us deeper into uncharted territory.

"What happened in the casino back there?" I asked. There was no reply. "It looked like you won a bunch of money. There were a lot of sevens flashing."

"I had a hunch and bet a bunch."

That was as much info as Lawrence was willing to part with, but it was just as well, because in Nevada you have to be twenty-one to collect your winnings.

We drove northeast through Mesquite, Nevada, and crossed the Arizona border, traveling across the northwestern tip of the state and into Utah. When we passed a sign that said St. George, Utah, was a few miles ahead, I told Lawrence it might be a good place to stop for gas and make another attempt to call his dad.

"No."

"Why not?"

"Parowan."

"Pair of what?" I said.

"Parowan, Utah." Not only was Lawrence good with numbers, but he was also a human road atlas. "Gas tank, two-hundred-mile range. Parowan, Utah, one hundred ninety miles from Vegas, baby. ETA three a.m. Mountain Daylight Time. More efficient. Stop there."

I'd managed to coax Lawrence out of his shell, at least for the moment. It was seventy miles to Parowan, so I took the opportunity to fill in the blanks that had developed since our unplanned two-man pilgrimage began.

"How'd you manage to hitch a ride?"

No answer. Lawrence plopped another piece of bubble gum into his mouth, increasing the size of his already-colossal gum wad exponentially.

"How about you write it down."

In what had already become a ritual of our journey, Lawrence wrote down his thoughts on a piece of paper, tore it out, folded it in half, and held it out for me, after which I suggested he read it aloud.

"Intercepted 7th Dimension communiqué from my bedroom. Entity knew you'd try to get to Kansas, but it was different this time, like it was showing us the way."

I remembered how one moment I was sitting confused at the curb, and the next moment the idea to "borrow" Wade's truck popped into my head. But that didn't explain how Lawrence had snuck into the back of the pickup.

"When did you jump in?

More scribbling, then Lawrence answered my question. "Packed my lunchbox and walked really fast to Rebecca's. Knew you'd go there to say goodbye before you left."

"How'd you know that?"

"Everyone knows," Lawrence said.

"Knows what?"

"You like her."

Was it that obvious?

"In case you don't know, it's obvious," Lawrence said.

For the first time in my budding friendship with Lawrence, I was the one who fell silent as I recalled how much it had hurt to see Brock Decker hanging out with my girl. Lawrence and I didn't say another word to each other the rest of the way to Parowan.

"You know the drill," I said as I handed Lawrence another five-dollar bill when we arrived at a gas station and convenience store off the highway.

I filled the tank as I watched Lawrence enter the phone

booth inside the store to call his father. No doubt Lawrence's dad had a bunch to say, because Lawrence did a lot of listening but not much talking. I couldn't help but wonder whether the Utah Highway Patrol would put out an all-points bulletin on Wade's pickup truck as we made a break for the Colorado border.

Lawrence hung up the phone, bought his dinner, and got back in the truck.

"What'd he say?"

"He's pissed. Said to turn around and come home."

I felt a lump forming in my throat. My hands got sweaty. "What'd you tell him?"

"Said I had plenty of gum," Lawrence replied, squinting. "Punch it."

Punch it? Where did that come from? Lawrence had a sense of purpose and a higher calling. He was developing into a normal teenager, opinionated and headstrong, right before my eyes. I steered the truck back onto eastbound Interstate 15.

"What's in the bag?" I asked.

"Dinner. Want some?"

Lawrence pulled out two packs of bubble gum and what looked like a large cup of coffee with a lid on it.

"Regular or decaf?"

Lawrence didn't answer. Instead, he opened his steel-plated lunch locker and took out a package of his go-to meal, freeze-dried chili mac 'n' beef. He dumped the lumpy substance into a bowl and poured in what he muttered was exactly one and three-quarter cups of hot water. Then he took out a spoon and stirred it.

"Need to let stand eight to nine minutes," Lawrence said.

We drove for another eight to nine minutes, then Lawrence declared it was suppertime and pulled a second spoon from the metal box.

"Twelve grams of protein, two hundred thirty calories per serving, thirty-three percent of the daily recommended allowance of sodium. Want some?"

It was the moment of truth. I'd seen Lawrence eat foil-wrapped brick food lots of times, but I'd never wanted to try it—until then. I lifted a spoonful of the steamy concoction and took a bite, not knowing what to expect. "Tastes like chicken."

That made Lawrence laugh. His laughter was brief and restrained, but the moment was a breakthrough, so I seized the opportunity to probe deeper. Curtis and Stretch and I had wondered why Lawrence ate the same freeze-dried chili mac 'n' beef every day. We weren't ones to talk, as we were equally guilty when it came to the familiarity and comfort of identical lunchtime meals. But Lawrence's choice was out of the mainstream.

"Was just wondering, what's the story with the freeze-dried stuff?" Familiar, deafening silence. "Sorry, that was kind of personal. Never mind."

Lawrence took his time finishing the stew. He topped it off with a double-decker dessert—two blocks of bubble gum—before scribbling another note and handing it to me. I unfolded it and pretended to read it out loud while I was driving: "'I think Stretch's peanut-butter-and-jelly sandwiches are gross, and Curtis's cream-cheese-and-sliced-pickle sandwiches on crust-deprived white bread make me want to hurl, and don't even get me started on Zeke's American cheese on egg bread with carrots curiously cut into goofy squared-off spears, because I prefer freeze-dried chili mac 'n' beef, because it's way more manly and delicious and tastes like chicken."

This time Lawrence laughed so hard that he spit out his wad of gum, pinning it to the windshield on the fly.

"Ouch, that's gonna leave a mark. Better not tell Wade," I said.

"I won't."

I gave Lawrence back his piece of paper and asked him to read it to me. There was another pause, but this time it wasn't because Lawrence was reluctant to read to me. He was waiting for Interstate 15 to intersect the western terminus of Interstate Highway 70 near Cove Fort. If we missed the I-70 turnoff, we might end up in Salt Lake City.

"Interstate 70, punch it," he said as he motioned toward the turnoff.

I negotiated the pickup across the transition lanes and onto Interstate 70, settling into the number-two lane. It was approaching 4:00 a.m. I asked Lawrence for our coordinates. He looked out the window to study the stars before using his pencil to draft a calculation.

"Distance one thousand sixty-nine miles, drive time sixteen hours, eighteen minutes, plus one hour for change of time zone. ETA eastern Kansas nine-fourteen p.m. Central Daylight Time."

That would leave plenty of time to convince the 7th Dimension to see things my way. All I needed after that was a good night's sleep to be ready for the tournament the next morning. I swung the conversation back to the secret of Lawrence's preference for freeze-dried food.

"What's the deal with the chili mac 'n' beef?"

Lawrence read from his piece of paper. "I'm in training."

"For what?"

There was more scribbling and reading: "To be the mathematics specialist on NASA's first manned flight to Mars. Need to prepare for spaceflight."

I knew there had to be something more to it than the twelve grams of protein per serving. Lawrence was a man with a plan.

"Also need a degree in applied mathematics. Going to apply to California Institute of Technology in Pasadena. After graduation from Caltech, have to pass NASA Class II space physical to be certified for spaceflight."

So Lawrence believed he was going to Mars one day. This brought to mind something Wade had written in one of his letters home after the marines deployed him to Central Asia: *You never know someone until you travel with him.*

Wade's letter went on to tell us about a fellow marine he didn't like at all when they first met. Wade said he came to understand the other guy a lot better after they shipped out and had to rely on each other. Now I began to understand what my brother had meant by those words. I was enjoying getting to know my quirky wingman on our strange odyssey.

Lawrence and I settled in as he calculated our next stop: Green River, Utah, 160 miles east. No doubt there were breathtaking cliffs and deep gorges dotting the Utah highway as we cut a path across the state, but daybreak was a couple of hours away, we were on a mission, and it was too dark to take in the beauty.

It was bitter cold outside, but the heater in Wade's old truck was working like a charm. We were crisp and toasty. For at least the next couple of hours, we didn't have a care in the world.

Check that.

I saw a row of bright blue and red flashing lights in the rearview mirror. A police siren accompanied the light show. I felt the familiar thumping of my heart as it rattled against my ribcage. It was the Utah Highway Patrol, signaling us to pull over.

23

It's Always Time to Take Action When There's Danger

I eased my foot off the gas, downshifted into second gear, and steered the pickup toward the shoulder of the highway. The brakes squealed in submission as our momentum carried us across piles of dirt and gravel that sent a cloud of dust wafting through the damp air. The truck slowed to a stop on the side of the road.

I pulled a Curtis Short and ceased breathing for a moment. Lawrence looked straight ahead and didn't utter a sound. The trooper pulled his cruiser behind us. He cut his engine and siren but not the row of bright lights. He exited the car, adjusted his belt, and walked toward us.

Clack-clack, clack!

The trooper banged on our window with the butt end of

his flashlight and motioned for me to roll it down. My hand trembled as I turned the hand crank.

"What seems to be the problem, officer?" I said, attempting to downplay the gravity of our predicament.

The trooper wore dark sunglasses even though it was pitch-black outside, and he wasn't smiling. The name, Chance Hunter, was etched onto his gold nameplate.

"You boys are a long way from California," State Trooper Hunter said.

"Yes, sir."

"You know you've got a taillight out?"

"No, sir."

"That's a safety hazard here in the Beehive State. License and registration, please."

I reached for the glove box as I wondered whether Central Utah Correctional Facility would serve freeze-dried food on Sundays. I fumbled through a mound of repair manuals and receipts until I found the vehicle registration and handed it to Trooper Hunter. He sized it up with a keen eye before delivering the bad news.

"Your vehicle registration expired five years ago."

"Yes, sir."

"Driver's license, please."

I knew the conversation would go from bad to worse when I handed Trooper Hunter my library card. He looked it over and frowned. "Wait right here."

"Yo, step on it!" For a kid who rarely said anything, Lawrence's words were a surprise, and his timing was awkward.

"Excuse me?" Trooper Hunter said.

"Don't mind him, sir, he's from out of state."

Trooper Hunter walked back to his cruiser. I watched through the side-view mirror as he reached into the car for the radio microphone and had an animated conversation with someone I assumed was a Utah Highway Patrol dispatcher. When he finished, he laid the microphone onto the front seat and unhooked two sets of silvery handcuffs from his belt.

"I'm afraid I'm going to have to ask you boys to step outside the vehicle."

Our gooses were cooked. I opened the Chevy's driver side door and stepped out onto the pavement. Lawrence didn't budge.

"C'mon, son, you need to come out of there right now."

I didn't know whether Lawrence had a problem with authority figures or was simply ignoring Trooper Hunter, but it didn't matter, because Trooper Hunter had had enough. He took one of the sets of handcuffs and clamped my right wrist to the Chevy's metal tailgate. Then he opened the passenger side door and reached in for Lawrence just as the loudspeaker on top of his cruiser crackled to life.

"Headquarters to twenty-one fifty."

Trooper Hunter released Lawrence's arm and rushed to the cruiser, keying his microphone. "Twenty-one fifty, go."

"Twenty-one fifty and all units in the vicinity, we've got a ten thirty-one crime in progress at Central Utah Basketball Equipment Company on Barkley Boulevard, unknown suspects seen removing palettes of basketball gear from the warehouse and loading them onto a panel truck with a large number seven painted on the side. All units respond with sirens and flashers, and use extreme caution."

Apparently, the 7th Dimension operated its own pick-up-and-delivery service.

"Ten-four, headquarters, twenty-one fifty responding."

Trooper Hunter slipped into his patrol car as he shouted instructions to us: "You boys stay right . . ."

I didn't know whether the trooper ever finished his sentence. The roar of the Chevy's engine drowned him out as Lawrence slid over to the driver's side and turned the key. When he revved the engine, I instinctively jumped into the back, wrenching my shooting hand because it was still cuffed to the tailgate.

Lawrence popped the clutch and fishtailed the pickup back onto the highway like an ex-convict fleeing a bank heist. Trooper Hunter drove down the rocky embankment, bounced his cruiser onto the access road, and raced away in the opposite direction.

Lawrence highballed it for two hours all the way to Green River as I shivered and hung on for dear life in the truck bed. It was daybreak when he finally pulled off the highway for gas. My teeth chattered as Lawrence drove up to a gas pump and cut the ignition. He climbed into the truck bed and retrieved Stretch's dad's bolt cutters.

Snap!

Lawrence sliced through the metal handcuff chain and freed me. My wrist was throbbing and still had a metal bracelet attached to it, but I was otherwise okay. The bolt cutters clanged on the truck bed when Lawrence tossed them back in.

"How'd you learn to drive like that?"

No answer. Lawrence got back into the passenger side of the truck and waited as I filled the tank. I topped it off, paid the cashier, and put us back onto Interstate 70, heading east.

"I need to know how you learned that."

"From watching you."

"You could've got us killed." No response. I was freezing and frazzled. I needed an answer. "Damn it, Lawrence, why'd you do that?"

Lawrence popped a bubble, reloaded, and popped another one.

"It's always time to take action when there's danger," he said.

It was hard to argue.

Lawrence, the rail-thin, gum-chewing, pencil-toting, high-functioning autistic math genius–astronaut-in-training–wunderkind had added one more virtue to his growing résumé.

He was Action Man.

24

Must've Been a Jayhawk

We drove for an hour across the easternmost part of Utah until we crossed the border into Colorado. I glanced at my watch: a few minutes short of 11:00 a.m.

"Coordinates, please."

Navigator Lawrence reached for his pad and scratched out the calculations.

"Drive time eleven hours, forty-two minutes, plus one hour for change of time zone. ETA eastern Kansas eleven thirty-seven p.m. Central Daylight Time. Next fuel stop: Silverthorne, Colorado."

We'd lost more than an hour overall but were still on schedule to arrive at the University of Kansas prior to the 7th Dimension's midnight deadline.

We were thirty miles outside Grand Junction, Colorado. I knew from geography class that Grand Junction lies at the western base of the Rocky Mountains. That meant we'd soon have to depend on Wade's antique truck to climb to an elevation of more than eleven thousand feet above sea level as we traveled through the Rockies, past Denver, and across the Great Plains into Kansas.

We'd left Los Angeles more than fifteen hours earlier. Except for Lawrence's brief stint as stunt-car-driver-in-training in Utah, I had been behind the wheel the entire time. I felt crusty from lack of sleep and was having trouble keeping my eyes open.

One peek at Action Man, and it was clear he was wide awake, although the big action had to be taking place between his ears, because he wasn't moving a muscle. I knew I couldn't count on him for spirited conversation, so I had to find another way to stay alert, because the alternative was careening Wade's prized possession into a rocky ravine two hundred feet beneath the interstate.

I reached for the chrome knob of the truck's AM radio and clicked it. Once the tubes warmed up, country music echoed from the speaker, a welcome departure from the high-pitched buzz of the Chevy's radial tires spinning across the highway.

After listening to a half dozen songs about pickup trucks and lost love, we were startled into full-alert status by a news bulletin breaking across the airwaves:

"You're tuned to AM 770, KQGJ in Grand Junction. This is news director Forrest Clare with a special report. We've just received a bulletin over the newswire that the Colorado State Patrol has put out an APB on a 1965 Chevrolet

Shortbed Fleetside pickup truck, sea-foam green, with California license plates. The vehicle is thought to be driven by a pair of juvenile delinquents who were involved in a serious altercation last night at World Famous Calvin's Gas, Food & Casino in Las Vegas. Law enforcement authorities believe that the suspects may be traveling eastbound on Interstate 70 across the Rocky Mountains toward Kansas. Authorities are asking for the public's help in locating the vehicle and bringing these fugitives to justice. KQGJ will bring you further developments as they occur. This is Forrest Clare reporting."

Serious altercation? Fugitives? All we had done was win a gigantic jackpot and then pretend we hadn't won it. Everywhere I turned, things were getting weirder and weirder. I began to wonder whether the 7th Dimension was working behind the scenes to test my sanity.

Whatever was going on, it was a genuine good-news/bad-news situation. The good news was, I no longer had a problem staying awake. The bad news was, I might need a bail bondsman. Every time a vehicle passed us on the highway, I wondered whether the driver had heard the news bulletin and recognized our highly recognizable vehicle.

If Lawrence was concerned, he didn't show it. He was as calm as Curtis Short standing at the free-throw line on the front end of a one-and-one. Lawrence went about his business of running the occasional calculation and snapping off bubbles at mile markers while I pondered all the homework I had piling up, especially a midterm assignment for my journalism class. There was nothing but time and interstate in front of us, so I asked Lawrence for an assist.

"Would you mind jotting down some notes on your pad for me?" He didn't answer but pulled a pencil from his pocket protector and sat up straight.

"*Never in the momentous history of basketball has there ever been a . . .* Erase that," I said. I started over. "*In a world where questions about basketball outnumbered the answers . . .*" Too dramatic. "Scratch that, too."

"Don't think," Lawrence said.

The math whiz had just given me unwanted advice on advanced journalism theory. All I needed him to do was sit quietly so I could think.

"Don't think," he said again.

"Perhaps you'd like to write this instead?"

"Don't think."

Just then I saw a bird land on the road ahead. I swerved to avoid it. Lawrence scribbled something onto his pad. Maybe it was more advice. He tore out the page, folded it in half, and handed it to me.

"Hello. Driving here. Read it to me, please."

"Must've been a jayhawk," he said, reading from the page.

A what? That was just great. I'd lost my train of thought. It felt like someone had let the air out of the ball. I was hungry and tired and cranky.

"Maybe I'm not cut out to be a journalist after all, but that's okay, because everything—besides ever playing college basketball, or ever hanging out again with my brother or my dad or my almost-future girlfriend—is still an option, and I didn't use to have options, but I guess I do now, and they include everything I don't want to do, including driving this dumb truck on this dumb highway to save this dumb game with this dumb kid—"

Smack!

What the—Lawrence had slapped me in the face. I was convinced he had done it as hard as he could too, because the side of my face felt like someone had lit it on fire.

"What'd you do that for?" I screamed.

"Don't think." I was thinking about hitting him back. "Write to the human heart."

I had no idea what he was talking about, but I started the story over again anyway. Lawrence wrote it all down:

> *"GRAND JUNCTION, COLO.—Little is known of his past. The present is unfolding before him on a lonely stretch of Mesa County interstate, the mile markers serving as roadside escort as they pace the journey. His future is yet to be written, though it holds much promise, as well as great challenge.*
>
> *"He goes by several names: the nerd in the back of the cafeteria, the large-brained one in math class, the pocket-protector prognosticator, or the Mars astronaut-in-training. His father calls him by his given name, Sherman, but his closest friends know him as Lawrence."*

I thought I saw Lawrence reveal a smile when I dictated that last part.

> *"Lawrence's odyssey into the unknown had been set into*

motion weeks earlier, when Ezekiel Archer committed an unnecessary and ill-timed act of violence during the city high school basketball championship, which resulted in Archer's expulsion from Southland Central High. He was subsequently banished, to serve out his final high school days at Ernest T. McDerney Continuation, where he met Lawrence and they became fast friends."

The friendship part had taken longer to develop than I was indicating, but I was using what writers refer to as narrative license to move the story along.

"Lawrence's quiet demeanor belies his true nature. He is a sensitive and intelligent young man with aspirations to be a part of the flight crew on NASA's first-ever manned expedition to the Red Planet, Mars.

"But before that can take place, there is much work to be done. Lawrence's classmates ridicule him for his pocket protector and the seven No. 2 pencils contained therein, but Lawrence uses those same pencils in conjunction with an ancient Greek geometric technique to reveal the secrets of an otherworldly force known as the 7th Dimension.

"When Lawrence learned of the 7th Dimension's plan to separate the game of basketball from its earthly bounds, he teamed up with Archer to travel to America's heartland in a modern-day two-on-one for the ultimate basketball title.

"Why would Lawrence risk everything by fighting for a cause not his own and engaging in a battle he surely could not win?

"'It's always time to take action when there's danger,' he says.

"There are still a few seconds left on the clock as Lawrence diagrams the final play he will use to defend the game brought to Earth for its power to promote peace and brotherhood among all who play it."

"What do you think? I asked. "Too epic?"

"I like my quote."

Newly energized, we drove on ahead and gassed the Chevy in Silverthorne as planned before setting sail for the Kansas state line 244 miles away. To get there, we had to continue along I-70 through Denver and follow the highway on its southeast trajectory to our next fuel stop, the small town of Flagler, Colorado, fifty-six miles from the Kansas border. It would be a relief to be free of checking the rearview mirror for Colorado State Patrol cruisers.

Traffic on the interstate was backed up as we arrived in Denver shortly before 2:30 p.m. We were already on a tight schedule. The last thing we needed was another delay. I asked Lawrence to run the numbers.

"We are five hundred sixty-five miles from eastern Kansas. Drive time eight hours, twenty-two minutes plus one hour for change of time zone. ETA University of Kansas eleven forty-nine p.m. Central Daylight Time.

Any more lost time and we'd miss the 7th Dimension's midnight deadline. I downshifted into second gear as traffic bunched up.

Then it happened.

Ka-chug, ka-chug, bang!

Wade's truck died, right there in the middle of the interstate. I pushed down on the clutch and turned the key, but nothing happened. Cars everywhere were honking at us to move out of the way.

"Take the wheel," I said. "I'm gonna push us. We need to get off the highway."

Lawrence slid over on the bench seat as I went to the rear of the truck and leaned against the bumper as hard as I could, but the Chevy wouldn't budge. Without thinking, I yelled for Lawrence to take his foot off the brake.

"I'm not an idiot," he shot back.

No question about that. My bad. I was steadying myself for another try when I heard a short blast from the siren of a Colorado State Patrol cruiser. The patrol car pulled behind the pickup and stopped. The trooper put on his hat and stepped outside, motioning me to join him.

I put my right hand into my pants pocket to conceal the handcuff. As I moved toward the trooper, I took stock of my situation. I had no driver's license, the truck's registration had expired five years before, and I'd put a fourteen-year-old kid behind the wheel. Then there was the capper: the Colorado State Patrol had an APB out on Wade's truck.

It had me wondering whether Colorado State Penitentiary in Cañon City would have a basketball hoop in the prison yard.

25

Does Wade Know You Borrowed His Truck?

The Colorado State Patrol trooper lit a fistful of road flares and laid them on the road to block traffic.

"C'mon, I'll help you push her off the road," the trooper said. He wasn't wearing a rectangular nameplate like Utah Highway Patrol Trooper Chase Hunter's, but his badge had the number 777 on it. He shouted instructions to Lawrence over the din of surrounding traffic. "Steer it off to a safe place on the shoulder."

If the trooper wondered why I was pushing the truck with my left hand while my right remained in my pocket, he didn't mention it. We got the Chevy moving fast enough for Lawrence to clear the ridge at the top of the gutter, and the truck came to rest a few feet off the interstate.

"You boys want me to call for a tow truck?" trooper whatever-his-name-was asked.

"No, sir."

"You need a ride to a repair shop?"

"No, sir, we'll take it from here."

"Suit yourself. You boys have a nice day."

The trooper scooped up the road flares and ground them into the pavement to extinguish them. The metaphor of something burning so brightly in one moment, only to be snuffed so completely out in the next, wasn't lost on me.

It was strange that Trooper 777 had never bothered to ask for my ID, but I let that go, because there was a more pressing issue at hand: we needed to travel 565 miles in a truck that was as dead as the game of basketball would soon be. We were finally out of options. I glanced at the sky in search of a sign, a miracle, anything.

Then it hit me.

Then it hit me again, squarely on the forehead as I stared off into space—cold, wet drops of rain, one after another, until I was standing in the middle of a downpour. Lawrence rolled up the driver side window as raindrops pinged off the truck.

I scrambled into the truck bed and pulled my jacket from my duffel bag. My mom always told me not to leave home without it. For once, I was glad I'd listened to her. I put it on and hoisted up the hood with my good hand so I could check the engine compartment for anything obvious. The only thing obvious was that I had no idea what I was looking for.

I got into the passenger side of the truck to escape the rain. When I put my hands inside my jacket pockets to warm them,

I was surprised to find a crumpled piece of paper. It was one of the envelopes my father had used to mail me a birthday card. I must have forgotten to take it out of my jacket when I got home from the bank after cashing the checks. I turned the envelope over. There on the back flap was my dad's address in Denver. We were running out of time and I was getting desperate.

"Cartographer, how do I get there?" I said to Lawrence as raindrops pounded the windshield.

Lawrence studied the address, penciled out the calculations, and pointed toward the northeast.

"15806 Stockton Street, three point five miles that way."

"Are you sure?"

"15806 Stockton Street, three point five miles that way."

That meant he was sure.

I retrieved my bike from the back. It was soaking wet, but at least the tires had air. I walked the bike to the driver side door and told Lawrence to roll down the window.

"You gonna be okay by yourself for a while?" Lawrence didn't answer, but he held up an unopened pack of bubble gum. "Cool. I'll be back before you know it."

I coasted down the next off-ramp and crossed under the freeway. The overpass shielded me from the wet weather for a moment, but the rain and the smell of wet asphalt hit me full force as I pedaled with everything I had. If anyone could get the truck running again, it was Wade or my dad. They'd restored it together from the chassis up and knew every inch of what was happening under the hood.

I wondered whether I could find my dad's house. Even if I

did, I had no idea if he would be home and if there would be enough time to get the truck running and over to eastern Kansas before the 7th Dimension's deadline. Then there was the problem of explaining to my dad, who I hadn't spoken to in five years, that I needed his help but couldn't tell him why, because of the promise I'd made to Lawrence.

The farther I rode, the harder it rained. After I'd gone a few miles, I rode up the driveway of a gas station and minimart to ask for directions. I went inside to the cashier's counter, where a frumpy woman glared in disapproval over the amount of water I'd tracked through the store.

The name sewn onto her blouse in red letters was Ruby. She had flaming-red hair held in place by ample amounts of hairspray. A long knitting needle, possibly for use as a weapon, transected it.

"Excuse me, ma'am, can you tell me where I can find 15806 Stockton Street?"

"Hello, friend. Who wants to know?" Ruby had answered my question with a question, so I knew the conversation would take longer than necessary.

"I do. I'm Zeke."

"That short for something?"

"Ezekiel."

"You going to buy anything, Ezekiel?"

I hadn't planned to, what with time running out on the game of basketball for all of humankind. I searched the candy section for Lawrence's favorite brand of bubble gum and put a pack onto the counter. Then I picked up a bottle of water from a rack by the cash register.

"That all you're going to buy?"

It was hard to tell what I was losing more of, time or patience. "I don't mean to be rude, Ruby, but I'm kind of in a hurry. Here's the money. Can you tell me where I can find 15806 Stockton Street?"

"Ezekiel Archer, you're just as impatient as your pappy."

"What? You know my dad?"

"That's his address. Comes in here all the time. Only thing Kenton Archer ever talks about is his two boys, Wade and Ezekiel. Figured you weren't Wade, seeing as though you're out of uniform."

I would have screamed if I thought it would have done any good. "Please tell me where I can find my dad."

"Two blocks yonder, make a right, third house on the left, the one with the basketball hoop over the garage. Can't miss it. Tell him I said hello, sweetie."

I followed Ruby's directions until I found the house as the rain intensified. There was a pickup truck in the driveway, a Chevy like Wade's, only several decades newer. I leaned my bike against a tree and shook the rainwater from my hair as I picked up the scent of wood burning in the fireplace. Butterflies did figure eights in my stomach as I approached the front door and rang the bell. I had no idea what I would say.

I heard rustling around inside. Then I saw a hand part the curtain covering the front window. A moment later, the front door opened, and out stepped my father.

"Zeke? My goodness, what are you doing here?"

I hadn't seen my dad in a long time. He looked a lot older and had put on a few pounds. His face bore several days of beard growth and the burden of his unexpected disappearance five years earlier.

"You're soaking wet. Come in and stand in front of the fire."

I walked inside. It was eerie seeing old photos of my brother and me on the walls of a place I'd never been to. "Your mother called. She said you and Curtis and Stretch were taking a bus to Kansas for some kind of basketball tournament. Where are they?"

Oh, they were on the bus, all right.

"I need your help."

"What is it, son?"

There were a lot of things I wanted to say to my dad, and there was a lot of stuff I couldn't tell him. "There's a problem with Wade's truck." I explained how I needed to get to the University of Kansas long before the bus would get me there, so I'd borrowed Wade's truck, but it had conked out on I-70 and I couldn't get it started.

"Your mother didn't tell me you got your license. Does Wade know you borrowed his truck?"

There were quite a few people asking me that question. "Can you help me get it started?"

"What kind of noise did it make when it died? Was it *ka-chug, ka-chug, bang*?"

Either my dad was psychic, or his knowledge of old Chevy engines was deeper than I'd realized. I nodded.

"Thought so. It's the carburetor. Kinda temperamental. You gotta treat her just so."

I put my bike in the back of my dad's truck while he went into the garage for his toolbox. He set it down in the truck bed and we took off for the highway. I told him I had a friend named Lawrence riding with me, and for the next five minutes or so, it was like old times back in Los Angeles.

"The bank called to make sure the checks were legit. Glad you finally cashed them."

I didn't want to tell my dad that I found the envelopes after putting them unopened into a cigar box in the back of my closet. A hard rain fell as we made our way to Wade's truck.

"When your mom called, she told me about Wade. You get any word on how his surgery went?"

"The marines said he made it through okay and is anxious to get out of the hospital."

There was no reaction from my dad. He was lost in thought when we pulled up behind the pickup. I remembered reading his letter of explanation a week earlier. I wondered whether our conversation had transported him back in time to events from the Iraq War he was trying to forget.

He cleared his throat as he found his focus. "I thought you said you had a friend traveling with you."

I looked inside Wade's truck. Lawrence was gone. "He was here a few minutes ago." He must have made a bubble-gum run.

I retrieved my bike and put it back in Wade's truck as my dad surveyed the contents of his toolbox. He pulled out a small screwdriver and a flat wooden stick that reminded me of going to the doctor for a sore throat.

"Hold the flashlight," he said, removing the air cleaner and using the stick to hold the carburetor choke plate open while he made adjustments to the throttle valve. "Give her a try." I pumped the clutch a couple of times and turned the key.

The engine chortled but didn't turn over. "Just need to find the right mixture of fuel and air," he said as he jiggled the metal parts. "Try it again."

I pushed down on the clutch and turned the key. The engine churned from side to side and backfired before clamoring back to life. With the engine idling, I stepped out of Wade's Chevy as my dad packed up his tools. When he came back to say goodbye, I thought he might have a lot to say, but there wasn't time.

"Listen, I'm sorry that I—"

"It's okay, Dad. We can talk about it some other time."

"I was going to ask where you got that handcuff, but I'm not sure I want to know."

His smile was warm and familiar. I hadn't seen it in a long time. It felt like home. My dad extended his arms and hugged me. I hung on for a long time as I tried to fill a hole in my heart that was five years wide. I thought about all the basketball games he'd never seen me compete in, and I wondered if I'd ever see him again. When I let go, my dad turned to walk away but stopped halfway to his truck. "Best of luck in the tournament, son."

He drove off as I noticed that Lawrence's metal lunch crate was gone. I was left to guess where he'd wandered off to, but I unraveled the mystery when I found a piece of paper folded in half on the dashboard:

Homesick. Miss my dad. Went home. Sorry.
Your friend,
Lawrence

26

The Cops Are Going to Arrest Us and Throw Away the Key

At least Lawrence had a dad to go home to.

Wade's truck was once again roadworthy, but that only meant I could turn it around and drive home. I would never make it to eastern Kansas in time. Even if I did, I had no chance of communicating with the 7th Dimension without the kid with the talking pencils.

The sick feeling in my stomach was the same one I'd had when we forfeited the city-title game. The only difference this time was I hadn't slugged anybody. It was time to go back to Los Angeles and take up a new sport, maybe cricket or lacrosse.

It was almost 4:00 p.m. I pulled back onto the highway and drove for the next exit, the same one I'd ridden my bike down before. When I got to the stop sign, I pulled off the road. There was no way I could drive home without Lawrence. I could just see it now: *"I'm really sorry about losing your son, sir. I don't know what happened. Lawrence, I mean Sherman, was there one moment and gone the next. It was the weirdest thing. I guess maybe he just vaporized, or something."*

I knew I had to search for him, so I made a mental list of the possible places he could have stopped to visit on his journey home. The local air and space museum, perchance? Maybe a bubble gum distribution warehouse? Perhaps a Denver-based freeze-dried brick food company?

Then it occurred to me that I was making things more complicated than they needed to be. Lawrence was a shortest-distance-between-two-points-is-a-straight-line kind of kid. That meant there was only one place he could be.

I crossed under the highway and got back on, heading west. I drove for five miles, exited, and got back on the interstate, traveling east. I crawled along the shoulder for a couple of hundred yards. Good grief, there he was, walking home at a brisk pace on the wrong side of the highway.

I pulled up alongside him, leaned over, and swung the passenger door open. "Get in." True to form, he kept walking, never looking up or breaking stride. Razor-sharp focus. I pulled the handbrake and left the engine running as I jogged after him. *"Lawrence, stop!"* I caught up and stepped in front of him.

"Get out of my way." Lawrence sounded angry.

"What are you going to do, slap me again?" I was beginning to lose my temper as well.

"Get out of my way!"

"You can't walk all the way home. You'll never make it."

"I know you don't care about me," he said. "You just left me there."

Lawrence reached into his pocket for another piece of gum. It was a good thing we had no plans to be anywhere, because it looked as though the conversation might take a while.

"I'm sorry it took so long to find my dad's place, and I care because I'm your friend. If you look up the word *friend* in the dictionary, it probably says, 'a person who is on good terms with another, bound or attached by personal regard.' That's us, buddy."

Then it hit me like the meteorite that had slammed into Chip's Sporting Goods: I was the first friend Lawrence had ever had. He didn't know what it was like to have one, so I had to lead by example. "Friends help friends out of a jam," I said. "That's why I have to get you home safe. Please get in the truck."

It took Lawrence several moments to process that last piece of information. I didn't know whether he applied a complex mathematical formula or simply accepted it at face value, but it didn't matter, because he turned around and walked back to the pickup.

I pulled the Chevy back onto the interstate and headed for the next exit, so I could get off and point us back in a westerly direction toward Los Angeles. Lawrence scratched out calculations on his pad as I approached the off-ramp.

"Keep going," he said.

I was confused, but I needed Lawrence to remain calm, so

I drove past the exit. There would be another one in a few miles, I reasoned. Lawrence continued writing, his pencil moving so swiftly across the page that it was a blur. When we approached the next off-ramp, he issued the identical command.

"Keep going."

"Why don't you tell me what's going on?" I said as the Chevy hurtled past the exit.

"Friends help friends out of a jam," Lawrence said.

"You need to give me more to go on than that." Lawrence wrote another note and held it out. "Hello, friend. Why don't you read it to me."

Lawrence unfolded the paper. "Five hundred sixty-five miles to eastern Kansas. Drive time six hours, thirty-nine minutes plus one hour for change of time zone. ETA University of Kansas eleven thirty-nine p.m. Central Daylight Time."

That couldn't be right. We'd lost an hour and a half of travel time when the truck broke down, but Lawrence had us arriving at the University of Kansas ten minutes earlier than before.

"Better check your math," I said. "It's flawed." That was what Lawrence had said to Mr. Appleton when the professor's formula was incorrect.

Lawrence didn't waver. "Equation valid. Contains one modification. Need to travel eighty-five miles per hour."

There were so many things wrong with Lawrence's strategy, I didn't know where to start. "There's no way we can drive that fast," I said. "There's too much traffic. Wade's truck is too old and can't handle it. The cops are going to arrest us and throw away the key. Your dad's gonna kill me, or I'm gonna get us killed, or worse—"

Smack!

Lawrence had slapped me in the face again, really hard, in the exact same spot as before.

"*Stop doing that!*" I screamed.

"Have to go eighty-six miles an hour now. Keep talking, soon it'll be eighty-seven."

The side of my face felt like it was covered in molten lava. My eyes were watering so much that the road was blurry. Lawrence was the only friend I had who had ever slapped me in the face, and now he had done it twice. He and I would have a serious conversation about it when the ordeal was finally over.

I mashed the gas pedal toward the floor. The Chevy picked up speed, and with it came more noise and vibration. I remembered Wade telling me the truck topped out at 125 miles per hour, so we still had breathing room, but we were pushing our luck.

"Flagler, Colorado, one hundred twenty-four miles ahead," Lawrence said. "Punch it."

27

What's the Deal with You and Brock?

The sun dipped below the horizon as we fueled up in Flagler and crossed the state line into Kansas. Adios, Colorado. *Vaya con Dios*. The Colorado State Patrol was no longer in charge of holding us responsible for every vehicle code infraction we committed. That job now fell to the Kansas Highway Patrol. Driving a "borrowed" antique truck at ultra-high speed across the Great Plains was guaranteed to draw unwanted attention.

Lawrence was riding shotgun, eyes fixed on the flat, barren road ahead. My head was pounding from the hundreds of miles we'd driven nonstop since leaving Los Angeles. I pushed hard on the accelerator to keep our speed above eighty-five miles per hour in hopes of staying ahead of schedule, while allowing for unknown trouble to unfold, which had happened regularly since we'd left World Famous Calvin's in Las Vegas.

I felt drowsy and rolled my window down, hoping a blast of cold air would give me a jolt of energy. The uncertainty about Wade's medical condition at the hospital in Germany left an empty feeling in my heart. I was still reconciling myself to the visit with my dad, an unwelcome reminder of how much I missed having him in my life, especially in those times when I had tough choices to sort out.

I wondered what Curtis and Stretch were up to as they rode the cushy Greyhound bus to a basketball tournament that would only take place if I could pull off the impossible. Then there was my mom, who had more questions than answers about Wade and me. I knew she must be worried beyond belief.

I tried not to think about Rebecca and the look of shock on her face when I had showed up at her front door unannounced, only to find that Brock Decker had beat me there. Rebecca was the closest I had ever come to having an actual girlfriend. I needed to get control of my feelings, or at least stuff them where they wouldn't occupy so much prime real estate in my brain.

I closed my eyes for a split second and filled my lungs with the truck cab's exhaust-tinged air. The next thing I knew, the top of my head slammed into the headliner as the truck nosedived down an embankment. Lawrence's blood-curdling scream pierced my right eardrum like a hot ice pick. My forehead rang off the steering wheel as the Chevy bounced and plummeted through tangled underbrush, finally coming to rest in a shower of dust on the access road below the highway.

Once everything stopped shaking, all I heard was silence, with the exception of my heart sledgehammering my ribcage. I took it as a good sign—it meant I was still alive.

"*Zeke!*" Lawrence's fingers dug into my shoulder and shook it. I opened my eyes but saw only stars. I guess I'd fallen asleep and driven us off the side of the road.

"What happened?" I said.

"You fell asleep and drove us off the side of the road."

At least that was settled.

It was pitch-black outside. I regained my senses and reached down to turn the key. The engine strained and rumbled but wouldn't turn over. I tried again. Nothing. I pounded my fist on the dashboard and wondered whether the 7th Dimension had set an over/under for the number of times I wanted to give up and go home. But there was too much on the line, and we had come too far to throw in the towel.

Lawrence raised the hood. I handed him Wade's flashlight and pulled out the air cleaner to expose the carburetor. Channeling my inner Kenton Archer, I held the choke plate open with my pocketknife and jiggled the throttle valve as Lawrence shined a beam of light into the engine compartment.

"Go give her a try," I said. Lawrence climbed into the cab and turned the key.

Tucka-thuck, tucka-thuck—vroooooooom!

"Want me to drive?"

During our odyssey to save the game, I'd learned that Lawrence did have a sense of humor, yet I was certain the question was a serious one. "It's okay, I've got this."

"Just kidding."

Good grief—just when you think you know a guy.

I put the truck back onto I-70, shifting into third gear and pushing the gas pedal to the floor until we hit eighty-eight miles per hour. We filled the tank twenty miles farther along in Ellis, Kansas, and got back onto the highway. I asked Lawrence to run the numbers again. He said we needed to maintain a speed of ninety miles per hour for another 185 miles to our last fuel stop in the small town of Alma, Kansas. From there, if we drove at ninety-five miles per hour for the final sixty-five miles to the university, we'd arrive at 7th Dimension world headquarters in Lawrence by 11:55 p.m.

"Cutting it kinda close, don't you think?" Lawrence didn't answer, but he didn't have to. There was no longer a margin of error. One more roadside calamity and my sports world would consist of badminton and table tennis. There was nothing but stark highway and the occasional vehicle traveling in the opposite direction as far as the eye could see, which wasn't far, because the sun had set hours ago and there weren't any streetlights.

I watched Lawrence out of the corner of my eye as he kept a vigil on the interstate ahead. He had developed into a respectable wingman on our journey into the nether Midwestern regions of the country. I thought Wade would be proud of me for looking after Lawrence and keeping him out of the crosshairs of bullies. I only hoped I could introduce Wade to Lawrence one day.

"What's the deal?" Lawrence said as he plopped another wedge of bubble gum into his mouth. It was a rare question from the kid. As usual, I had no idea what he was talking about, so I decided to do what Ruby in Denver would do in a similar situation—I answered his question with a question.

"What in the world are you talking about?"

"What's the deal with you and Brock?"

This was no time to indulge in a compare-and-contrast exercise on my relationship with Brock Decker, past and present. "Do me a favor and just watch the road."

"What's the deal with you and Brock?"

What Lawrence lacked in timing, he made up for in peskiness. "It's not a very interesting story, and I really don't think this is the—"

"What's the deal?"

Lawrence was agitated and wasn't letting it go. Since I had no interest in getting my face slapped again, I gave him the short version of my chronological history with Brock.

"Met him a long time ago," I said. "We were good friends, then one day we weren't. Now leave me alone."

There was scant light in the truck cab, but enough to see Lawrence rear back and swing his palm toward my face. I sprung my right hand off the steering wheel to catch his wrist in midflight, but I overcompensated with my left and lost control of the vehicle.

My life flashed before me as Wade's prized Chevy rocketed sideways down the highway at ninety miles per hour, tires smoking like a peat fire.

The prospect of an open-casket funeral seemed unlikely.

28

You're an Idiot

I had been on Earth for seventeen short years. There was lots of stuff I hadn't done, like score fifty points in a game or celebrate my eighteenth birthday, so I wasn't quite ready to clock out.

The Chevy's transmission screamed in protest when I jammed the gearshift lever into second in an attempt to slow down and regain control. The change of momentum caused the pickup to spin around on the pavement like a wobble-stone top. We nearly flipped over before screeching to a halt in the center of the interstate facing the wrong way. Then we cheated death for the second time within a matter of seconds when an eighteen-wheeler, its air horn shrieking, buzzed past us just inches away. I had to decide between lecturing Lawrence on proper friendship protocol or pointing us toward the University of Kansas and stepping on the gas pedal.

"You and I are going to have a serious talk if we ever get out of this mess," I said as I swung the truck around and took it back to ninety miles per hour. I thought about asking Lawrence to update the math but decided against it—the less he said for the rest of the trip, the better.

"What's the deal?"

"The deal is, if you ask me about Brock one more time, I'm going to stab you in the leg with one of your seven pencils." No doubt fatigue had set in. If I were in my right mind, I would have realized that plunging a pencil into Lawrence's femur would leave us with only six working pencils, and that wouldn't get it done with the 7th Dimension.

Lawrence sat in silence after that. A few miles later, when headlamps from a westbound vehicle flashed through the windshield, I saw a tear glistening on his cheek. Up until then, the only emotion Lawrence had displayed was anger. This was fear and sadness. I tried to ease the mood.

"Just kidding. No way I would do that. There wouldn't be enough time to apply a tourniquet to your thigh and still make it to the University of Kansas in time, and if you passed out from loss of blood, there wouldn't be anyone left in the truck to slap me senseless."

No reaction. Lawrence had a high comedic threshold. It was time to break out my A material.

"I'd have to stab you with the other six pencils in a heptagonal configuration using the ancient geek-ometric technique of neurosis contusion. That's too dangerous to attempt while driving at such an unsafe speed."

That one broke through. Lawrence grinned and wiped his

eyes with his sleeve while I peeked at the instrument panel. The temperature gauge said the water temp was on the rise, but Lawrence distracted me from it.

"What's the deal?"

I needed Lawrence to remain calm, even if keeping him that way meant confronting a somber memory from my past, so I decided to tell him what had happened. "Met Brock a long time ago in park league basketball. Parents signed us up. We were teammates."

I explained to Lawrence that Brock and I did everything together after that—birthday parties, sports events, father-son trips, the works. We were best friends, inseparable. Then one day I was playing pickup basketball at the rec center with Curtis and Stretch when Brock showed up with this girl.

"Brock introduced her as his stepsister," I said. "He wanted us to let her play. Said she was pretty good, but I was going through my he-man, tough-guy phase and wasn't having it."

"Need some gum?" Lawrence seemed to sense my reluctance to continue with the story.

"Nah, I'm good."

I explained that Brock forced the issue, so I agreed to let her join us. Brock and I chose teams and, naturally, he picked his stepsister and I selected Curtis and Stretch. I decided to guard Brock's stepsister to teach her something about playing hoops with the big boys. A couple of minutes into the game, I boxed her out and went up for a rebound. When I came down with the ball, she tried to swat it out of my hands, so I flailed my elbows to protect it.

"Nailed her right smack on the nose, fractured it on the spot," I said. "Blood everywhere. Rumor was you could hear it crack all the way on the other side of Bird Parkway."

Lawrence stopped chewing. His jaw loosened and a wad of pink gum fell into his lap. "Then what happened?"

The Chevy thumped and shuddered over a pothole as I filled in Lawrence on the rest of the details. "Brock got real angry. Lots of pushing and shoving before Mr. Shields ran out from his office to break it up. It was an accident, pretty much, but Brock insisted I'd done it on purpose. That was the end of our friendship."

"Was she okay?"

"Guess so. Never saw her again after that. I think her name was Betty or Betsy or Becky or something."

Crap.

"*Holy crap!* Becky is Rebecca Tuesday. I broke the nose of my future almost-girlfriend."

"Whoa."

When I met Rebecca at McDerney, I thought she looked familiar, but I didn't put it together even though the signs were there. When I saw Brock inside her house, I assumed he was busting a move on my girl, when he was only there visiting his stepsister and maybe even telling her what a great guy I was. Geez, I felt like an idiot.

"You're an idiot," Lawrence said, proving that even a blind man knows when the sun is shining.

I wanted to turn the truck around so I could race home and square everything with Rebecca and Brock, but first I had to save the game of basketball for all of humanity. A muffled explosion jolted the truck cab, shattering those plans. The needle inside the temperature gauge danced in the red as steam poured out from under the hood. Wade's relic on four wheels had finally succumbed to the mercy rule. It hissed and groaned as I steered it onto the shoulder of the highway and cut the ignition.

There was no light outside and not enough time to fix this mess.

29

You'll Never Take Us Alive!

We were in the middle of nowhere in northeastern Kansas. It was silent, so long as you didn't count the fizzling steam escaping from our overheated radiator. The sweet but toxic smell of boiling-hot engine coolant filled the cab. I was too despondent to feel sorry for myself but still had enough sense to crank down my window.

"Need to optimize the path of air by creating a natural breeze channel," Lawrence said as he rolled down his passenger side window. Lawrence had a clear understanding of the concept of cross-ventilation. "Need to find the source of the leak and cap it." He also had a keen sense of the principles of fluid dynamics.

When we opened the hood, the column of steam dissipated, revealing a hole in the main radiator hose. Lawrence went back to the cab and retrieved a roll of black electrical tape that Wade kept in the glove compartment. He must have noticed it when I had rummaged around in there to find Wade's registration back in Utah. There was no reason to think it could seal a hot and leaky radiator hose, but we had to try.

I needed to remove the radiator cap to release pressure so we could patch the hose. Using my jacket as an oven mitt, I pushed down on the cap and turned it, but the pressure blew it off and shot boiling antifreeze onto my hand, scalding it. My body shuddered from the pain. It was my shooting hand, the same one I'd bloodied breaking my fall when the meteorite struck Chip's. It was also the same hand that was connected to the wrist I'd wrenched when we evaded arrest in Utah.

"That's going to leave a mark," Lawrence said as blisters formed on my palm. I couldn't tell if he was trying to lighten the moment or simply stating a fact, but I was in too much pain to make the call.

When steam stopped drifting from the hose, Lawrence wrapped the entire roll of tape around the leak. I went inside the truck to get the bottle of water I'd bought at the minimart in Denver. I poured its precious contents into the filler neck. It wasn't nearly enough to fill the radiator, but it was everything we had. I reattached the cap with my good hand and dropped the hood.

"Gimme the keys," Lawrence said.

"No way." If he thought I would let him drive, he was out of his mind.

"Gimme the keys," Lawrence said, more insistent than before.

"No."

"Can't drive with that hand. Gimme the keys."

Lawrence was right. I could steer the pickup with my left hand, but there was no way I could operate the Chevy's three-on-the-tree gearshift with a hand that felt as if someone had shoved it into a volcano. Against my better judgment, I handed Lawrence the keys.

"Get in," he said.

I wondered what TV show Lawrence had watched, in which the star states the obvious like that, as if I'd still be standing there as he drove away if he hadn't instructed me to get in. It was gratifying to watch him gain confidence as we ventured deeper into the unknown.

Lawrence put the truck back on the highway and floored it. The temperature gauge told me the engine was running hot, but the electrical tape had done the trick. We needed to get to Alma for our final fuel stop before doing a four-wheel lock skid into a KU parking lot. I was afraid to look at the speedometer because I didn't want to know how fast we had to travel to make up for lost time.

"Gotta go a hundred and five miles per hour," Lawrence said.

Yikes, the wisecracking psychic stunt car driver must have sensed my question. "I thought you had to figure that stuff out on a piece of paper."

"I do calculations in my head and only use pencil and paper so people won't think I'm weird."

That ship had sailed and we were on the open seas by then. I watched as the speedometer needle hit 90 miles per hour and kept going—95, 100, 105. The temperature gauge nipped at the red zone but did not cross into it. Lawrence never missed a beat at the mile markers, but the gum-snap intervals were shorter than before. There were few cars on the highway that late at night. Whenever drivers saw us barreling down the highway, they moved to the right to let us pass.

My hand ached from what must have been a second-degree burn. My head ached from everything else. Lawrence was the picture of focus, hands at ten and two, eyes locked onto the road. The cab's interior hummed and vibrated but was otherwise tranquil. I needed to make sure Lawrence remained alert, so I bounce-passed a question.

"How did you end up at McDerney?" No response. There was an outside chance Lawrence had fallen asleep with his eyes open, but the smart money was on him just ignoring me again. "What happened? You slug somebody?" The velocity of Lawrence's gum chewing increased with each question. "Better seating in the cafeteria? Vice Principal Littwack is your uncle?"

"I killed someone."

The hairs on the back of my neck stood at attention. Horrible accident? Case of mistaken identity? Cold-blooded murder? Maybe I shouldn't have pressed so hard. I thought I had Lawrence figured out, but this new information was making me wonder if I knew him at all.

"Just kidding. I used to say that at my other school so people would leave me alone."

"How'd that work out for you?"

"Everyone left me alone."

Lawrence's tactic for insulating himself from the outside

world was as direct as his route to the 7th Dimension's eastern Kansas command post.

"It's just you and me and this lonesome stretch of highway. Your secret is safe with me. What happened?"

Lawrence said that things hadn't worked out at a series of public schools before his mother enrolled him in a private institution for special needs kids.

"No one understood me there, so I stayed inside my own head and never ever came out."

Lawrence told me he began to obsess about getting aboard the first manned flight to Mars after reading about NASA's successful Mariner 4 flyby mission to the Red Planet, but he never told anyone about his goal.

"Got good grades in math, flunked everything else. School administrators thought I couldn't be saved. Mom didn't know what to do, so she killed herself. Found her on the kitchen floor when I got home from school."

Lawrence had the truck up to 108 miles per hour when he told me that last part. His hands were steady on the wheel. Mine were trembling. One day earlier, when I'd gone to Lawrence's house, I'd only met his father. I'd wondered about his mother. Mystery over. I felt lucky to have both of my parents—even if my dad was no longer in the picture. I wondered whether that would change after seeing him in Denver.

"Sorry, man. I didn't know."

"Next day at school, everyone knew. Was in the cafeteria eating freeze-dried chili mac 'n' beef. Kid comes up to me, says it's my fault my mom offed herself."

"What'd you do?"

"Slapped him so hard, kids were saying you could see my handprint on his face till the end of fifth period. Saw him in sixth-period calculus class, slapped him harder."

Lawrence said that the next day he was expelled. The only school that would take him in after the Slaps Heard 'Round the World was McDerney.

"I like the cafeteria there. Lots of space for my lunch gear and math books."

I had it on good authority that NASA maintained a strict no-slapping policy in space, so Lawrence's future seemed bright, so long as he could restrain himself when angry.

Another glance at the speedometer revealed that Lawrence now had Wade's Chevy searing a path across the Kansas heartland at 110 miles per hour. I knew he ran the numbers in his head every time he popped a mile-marker bubble, tailoring our speed for an eventual 11:55 p.m. arrival at interdimensional Entity base camp.

A police siren and flashing red light atop a Crown Victoria broke the relative calm five miles outside Alma. It seemed only fair that a Kansas Highway Patrol law enforcement officer should have a crack at us after we had evaded arrest in California, Nevada, Utah, and Colorado.

I made a mental list of the people I'd have to apologize to when I returned home after doing time in the big house. Lawrence had other plans. Rather than ease off the accelerator pedal, he pushed it to the floorboard. The kid had Wade's monument to mid-sixties automotive engineering up to 120 miles per hour.

"See you in hell, copper!" Lawrence screamed at the top of his lungs. "You'll never take us alive!"

It was a line of dialogue from as many B-movies Lawrence had watched on late-night TV as there were state prisons in Kansas.

30

C'mon, Grab Your Pencils

We barreled right past the small town of Alma at 125 miles per hour. The Kansas Highway Patrol cruiser was glued to our tail, siren wailing. Alma was supposed to be our final fuel stop, but the math of on-time arrival at 7th Dimension headquarters supported taking our chances on a near-empty gas tank over guaranteed incarceration.

Lawrence seemed serious about not wanting to be taken alive. He would either outrun the law or die trying in a quarter-mile trail of molten roadkill. The speedometer only went up to 125, but the Chevy's V8 engine nudged the needle into unoccupied no-man's-land beyond it.

Lawrence struggled to maintain control every time the pickup thumped a section of uneven pavement. Then without warning, we hit an upward incline in the road and went airborne into the darkness. My stomach lurched into my throat as we dropped from the sky and our four tires skidded back onto the highway. The truck swerved in protest, but Lawrence coaxed it back into line.

My throat tightened in fear. I strained to speak. "That's enough. It's not worth it."

Lawrence rebuked the notion without hesitation. "Dude, it's basketball. It's always worth it."

I recalled that Curtis had said those exact words, even the "dude" part, when I suggested we concede after he sprained his ankle in the three-on-three tournament at Jefferson. Lawrence had been in the crowd that day and must have overheard us.

"C'mon, man," I said. "That's enough. You're gonna get us killed."

I estimated we were going at least 130 miles per hour, but there was no way to know for sure. Lawrence used his thumb to motion to the rear of the truck. I turned around to see the cruiser decelerate and pull over to the side of the road. Maybe the law enforcement officer had given up, or maybe it was a trap to lull us into a false sense of security while the Kansas Highway Patrol set up a roadblock a few miles ahead. Lawrence slowed down to a 120-miles-per-hour snail's pace and flipped another piece of bubble gum into his mouth.

It was freezing outside. Inside the truck cab, sweat poured from my head as if I were sitting in a sauna. My nostrils stung from the smell of boiling coolant. The temperature gauge was parked in the red. I glanced at my watch: 11:25 p.m. I looked across the dashboard and squinted to see the fuel gauge.

We were on empty.

"I need the numbers," I said.

No response. Lawrence was in the zone.

"I need to know if we're going to make it."

Still nothing. Time was running out. If there was no hope of arriving before the deadline, I wanted to know, so I could prepare myself for failure. I needed to get Lawrence's attention. "Talk to me or I'm going to slap you really hard with my bad hand."

"Sixty miles, drive time thirty minutes. ETA University of Kansas eleven fifty-five p.m. Central Daylight Time."

I still had a shot at saving the game, but Lawrence hadn't mentioned our fuel level. I was worried we wouldn't have enough to make it. "What about our gas?"

Lawrence snapped a bubble. "What about it?"

"Is there enough?"

"Maybe."

"Maybe?"

"Yeah, maybe," Lawrence said.

It was unusual for Lawrence to be unsure of the numbers. My insides quivered and twitched. "Can you be more specific?"

"Alma fuel-stop calculation was conservative. I based it on engine efficiency, speed, altitude, weather conditions, road topography."

"Do we have enough gas to make it to the university?"

"Maybe."

We were back where we started. Lawrence was good with numbers, but this was out of his hands. Mine too. No margin for error. Nothing left to do but ride it out and ponder the ifs. Like, if the truck didn't break down. If Lawrence didn't catapult us into a ravine. If the Kansas Highway Patrol didn't lay a spike strip across the highway ahead. If we didn't run out of gas. If all those things didn't happen, we had a shot at arriving in time to save the game.

I chewed on the fingernails of my good hand as the kid blazed a trail through Paxico, Maple Hill, Topeka, Tecumseh, and Lecompton before arriving at the outskirts of his namesake town, Lawrence, Kansas. Lawrence the Kid eased off the gas and slowed to ninety miles per hour as we blew through a half dozen tollbooths. We took the southbound McDonald Drive exit on two wheels, tires screeching at seventy-five miles per hour. A sign at the bottom of the off-ramp said it was three miles to the university.

I checked the time: 11:52 p.m. Small wonder Lawrence aspired to be an intergalactic mathematics specialist. He'd totally nailed the calculation. We had three minutes to make it to the grove of trees adjacent to Allen Fieldhouse that served as 7th Dimension headquarters. The five-minute buffer before the midnight deadline was all I needed to make my case for basketball to remain where it was.

Lawrence shot down McDonald Drive for a half mile and eased onto Iowa Street. After another mile and a half, the unexpected happened. Or maybe it was the fully expected, what with all the roadblocks that had appeared in my path since I'd walloped an innocent basketball referee.

The Chevy bucked and sputtered about a mile short of its destination. Lawrence pumped the clutch and threw the transmission into neutral, hoping to coast the rest of the way to campus. No such luck. The pickup hacked and wheezed one final time. Then it ran out of gas. It was a merciful death, a welcome relief from the fierce attack of heat and sound generated by Lawrence's pushing the engine to its limits. He steered the Chevy to the curb. When it had rolled to a stop, he pulled the handbrake, turned off the ignition switch, and handed me the key.

"I'm done with this," Lawrence said. "You can have it back."

I interpreted the gesture as a noble mathematician's final act of concession. Lawrence had honored the additive property of equality by adding the same quantity to both sides of an equation in order to maintain its balance: first he had demanded the keys, and then he had given them back.

It was 11:54. The ball was in my court. I'd traveled halfway across the country on an improbable one-on-seven fast break to take the rock to the otherworldly rack. If I couldn't score, I'd at least try to get to the free-throw line to shoot a pair.

I attempted to fist-bump Lawrence and missed. I caught a piece of his fist on the backswing, good enough for both of us. "Wait here, I'll be right back."

Lawrence didn't look me in the eye and didn't respond. I got out of the truck and took a look around. The air was chilly, the street was empty, and the sky was black, but streetlights led the way to campus. I used my good hand to pull my bike and duffel bag from the truck bed. When I straddled the bike frame and gripped the handlebars, I almost passed out from the sharp pain that shot through my right hand. I cranked the pedals with every ounce of strength I had left.

Half a block later, I squeezed the handbrakes and skidded to a stop. I didn't know if the cause was sleep deprivation or lack of food and water, but I'd forgotten about the most important part of reasoning with the 7th Dimension: Lawrence. I needed the kid with the pencils to set the most important pick of my life. I raced back to the truck and banged on Lawrence's window. He rolled it down. It was 11:55.

"That was fast. How'd it go?" Lawrence flashed a split-second micro-grin, an ill-timed but welcome first-ever attempt at humor in my presence.

"Be glad I'm not Curtis. He would've slugged you," I said. "Gotta make a run for it. Grab your pencils."

I put my bike back into the truck bed as Lawrence pulled his aluminum crate from inside the cab. Rather than extract the pencils, he picked up the crate by the handle and turned to race-walk toward the university. It was 11:56.

"We can't take that with us. Too heavy. Gotta leave it and run or we'll never make it." Lawrence ignored me and continued to race-walk. I ran to catch up with him.

"I can't leave it here," he said. "I need to have it with me."

I had no idea why Lawrence needed to take along his case, but I'd been around him long enough to know this wouldn't end well if he didn't get his way. With my duffel slung over my shoulder, I picked up the case with my good hand and headed toward destiny, Lawrence heel-toeing stride-for-stride alongside.

It was 11:57. Morocco's Hicham El Guerrouj, who holds the world record in the mile with a time of 3 minutes, 43.13 seconds, would've arrived at 7th Dimension headquarters about a minute past midnight. Unless we sprouted wings and took flight, it was unlikely we would arrive before then.

31

I Think I'm Picking Up Something

Lugging Lawrence's metal case down Iowa Street was like hauling a piano up a flight of stairs. When we stopped at the West 15th Street intersection, I dropped to one knee to catch my breath. Lawrence studied the stars and motioned for a left turn. No way I was going to check my watch. It would only be bad news.

We heaved and staggered down West 15th Street until we saw it: a wooden post embedded in a circular chunk of concrete in the grass. Attached at the top were two blue street signs: NAISMITH DRIVE, ALLEN FIELDHOUSE DRIVE.

We'd made it to the outskirts of 7th Dimension territory.

I checked my watch, though my heart wasn't in it. No luck. 12:05 a.m., as in five minutes past basketball. No surprise that I was five minutes late again. It was the story of my life. I'd traveled halfway across the country for the chance to undo my biggest mistake, and the only thing I had to show for it was an interdimensional tardy lockout.

I felt the tingling sensation of tears rolling down my cheeks. I didn't want Lawrence to see me cry, so I turned away—it was my turn to ignore *him*. Living in a world without basketball was too much to think about. Knowing it was all my fault made it unbearable.

Deadlines exist so stuff can get done. The 7th Dimension's deadline was the most important of my life, and I'd blown it. It wasn't the first time I missed zero hour, but in the past I'd managed to wiggle out of trouble by asking for an exception. I dried my eyes and turned to ask Lawrence if there was still a chance, but he was gone.

"Lawrence!" I called out. No response, which was standard for the pencil maven. I set out to track him down, stopping first at the main entrance to Allen Fieldhouse along the arena's exterior walkway. The lights inside were out and I couldn't see any movement through the windows, so I headed north on the walkway until I noticed the silhouette of trees against the night sky. As I drew closer, I saw Lawrence under those trees crouching on the grass.

"You can't just walk away like that. I've been looking all over for you," I said, before noticing that Lawrence was hovering over seven No. 2 pencils interconnected in a heptagonal configuration on the ground. Then it hit me: the root system under that tiny grove of oak, sycamore, and pine trees was 7th Dimension headquarters.

We were standing at ground zero.

"What are you—"

Lawrence threw up a hand to silence me but did not break his concentration. He stood and rotated his head on its axis as if adjusting the tuning knob of a radio to lock it onto a station. When he found the right position, he froze and closed his eyes.

"I think I'm picking up something," he said.

32

It Was Now or Never

I stepped back to give Lawrence room to operate. His face contorted and his body vibrated in the cold, damp air. I had no clue about the information he was receiving, or if it even mattered.

I grew impatient after standing around for a while. "What's going on?"

Lawrence dropped to his knees but maintained the angle of his head. "The Entity says you should brush up on your checkers."

Not chess. Checkers. That must be what rock bottom looked like.

I shook my head in disbelief over the insanity of what was unfolding before my eyes. I was standing in a grove of trees in the middle of the night 1,600 miles from home with a fourteen-year-old autistic kid who was having an alternate-reality contact experience with an interdimensional energy being that had an unstoppable midrange jumper.

Lawrence collapsed onto the ground in the fetal position. It looked as though the communication link with the 7th Dimension had been severed. It was the beginning of figuring out how to put my life back together in Los Angeles in the wake of basketball's exodus from Earth.

I helped Lawrence to his feet. His clothes were damp from the grass and he was shivering. I took off my jacket and wrapped it around his shoulders. The kid had risked his life for me. That was the true measure of friendship, to put someone else's well-being before your own. I would never forget it.

"You good? I was a little worried about you."

"Entity didn't want to violate its prime directive of noninterference but was forced to because it didn't anticipate your courage and commitment," Lawrence said. "It didn't think you'd show."

To be fair, I didn't think the Entity would show. It didn't owe me a damn thing. I'd made the poor choices that had pinned the 7th Dimension into a corner. It was only doing what it thought was best for the world. I had to live with the consequences, even if it meant I'd play a lot of shuffleboard at the rec center when I got home.

Lawrence packed his seven pencils back into his portable metal locker and snapped it shut. I wondered why he'd made me run an entire mile carrying that boat anchor when it only contained pencils and a lunch kit. I asked him, and he answered my question with a question.

"How else am I supposed to carry my stuff around?"

Lawrence lived by a set of rules and logic all his own. As with any friend, you embraced the good with the interesting.

"Let's go home," I said as I picked up my duffel bag and Lawrence's metal case and began the slow journey back to the Chevy, retracing my steps along the arena's walkway toward Naismith Drive. As we approached the entrance to Allen Fieldhouse, I noticed that the lights inside were on.

Basketball fans around the world know that Allen Fieldhouse is named after the legendary University of Kansas Coach Forrest Clare "Phog" Allen, who led the KU men's basketball program for thirty-nine seasons. During that time, he won twenty-four conference championships and three national titles. Allen was a disciple of Dr. James Naismith, the inventor of the game. Allen Fieldhouse was supposed to be my basketball home for the next four years, but that had changed when the university withdrew my scholarship.

I had only seen the inside of the arena in televised basketball games. I walked up to the main door. I figured I would never be there again, so it was my only chance to see the court firsthand. I set down the baggage and reached for the metal door handle. It was unlocked.

Lawrence and I slipped inside and took a look around. We expected to be greeted by security guards but instead stumbled upon a museum dedicated to the history of Kansas basketball: old equipment, uniforms, bios, and photos of players from the earliest days of the sport.

I went back for my duffel bag and pulled out the basketball I'd bought at Chip's Sporting Goods before a fragment of 7th Dimension space rock slashed through Chip's roof.

"You up for checking out the court?" I said. No answer from Lawrence. That either meant yes, no, or maybe. "Let's go. I'll play you one-on-one to see who gets to lug your lunch-box back to the pickup."

"I'll wait here and guard our stuff."

"Suit yourself. Don't wander off."

I tucked my ball under my arm and walked through the interior of Allen Fieldhouse until I came to a doorway leading to the basketball arena. I turned the handle. For the second time in a row, a door that by all rights should be locked, wasn't. I opened it and made my way down a corridor. When I reached the arena, I stood on the concourse and filled my lungs.

The feeling reminded me of the first time I ever walked into a basketball gymnasium in Los Angeles. It was a park league, and I was seven years old. Back then, that old gym was the size of a shoebox, with hardwood floors that were battered and endless.

The arena in Allen Fieldhouse emanated a more complex aura, a mixture of sweat, pain, grace under pressure, jubilation, heartbreak, friendship, hope, the wonderment of a properly executed fast break, and the ethereal magic of teamwork. It must be what park league basketball smelled like in heaven.

The arena was dimly lit, but the colors were vibrant. There were orderly rows of blue, red, and gold seats constructed of wood. Silky banners lined the rafters, evidence of five national championships and countless conference titles and NCAA final-four appearances.

A colorful cartoon bird was painted onto the floor at

center court, surrounded top and bottom by the words KANSAS JAYHAWKS and ALLEN FIELDHOUSE.

Jayhawks?

Hadn't Lawrence said it was a jayhawk that had landed in front of us on the highway outside Grand Junction? What was a mythical avian Kansas mascot doing in the middle of a Colorado interstate? If I'd run over the bird instead of swerving to avoid it, would that have been the 7th Dimension's way of telling me to give up and go home, because I'd already killed the game?

My sense of wonder morphed into waves of despair, not so much for my blown opportunity to be a part of the basketball program at KU, but for the world's loss of a popular game so rich in history. It was a textbook example of cause and effect: my actions in the city finals had served as the tipping point for the 7th Dimension's ultimate decision. I knew I would have to live with the outcome. It left a heavy feeling in my heart.

I bounced my basketball a couple of times on the concourse's concrete floor with my left hand. The leathery *thump-thump* echoed across the arena. I walked down the steps all the way to the sidelines. I noticed the arena didn't have multiple half-courts set up for three-on-three tournament play, just the main court in the center of the arena with a hoop at either end.

I imagined that the Entity's decommissioning of basketball would be a labor-intensive operation involving lots of panel trucks with large number sevens painted on the sides. Maybe the 7th Dimension would start in outlying areas around the globe before making its way here to the birthplace of the game to shutter it. I still had my ball, but I wasn't sure why.

I scanned the arena. Not a soul in sight. It was now or never.

I spun my ball on my index finger as I walked onto the court, stopping at one of the free-throw lines. I closed my eyes and imagined Wade dispensing advice on the mechanics and psychology of free-throw shooting.

"Knee, elbow, wrist," he would tell me. *"See the ball go through the hoop in your mind's eye before you release it."*

I opened my eyes and bounced the basketball a few times with my blistered right hand. A sharp pain ran up and down my arm as I took a deep breath, exhaled, and found my center of gravity. Then I shot the ball.

Whoosh.

There isn't a sweeter sound in the world.

What I heard next, however, sent shivers down my spine. It was a voice that seemed to come from the center of the earth.

"Young man, you should not be in here."

33

I Summoned My Last Ounce of Courage

I felt the blood drain from my face. I realized my injured right hand was trembling when I swept the back of it across my forehead to wipe away the cold sweat. My ball thumped unattended in a succession of increasingly smaller and faster bounces until it settled on the floor under the basket.

There had been a police presence on every leg of this wild journey. It was clear I was trespassing, and my illicit visit to Allen Fieldhouse had attracted the authorities. I needed to decide what to do next. Make a run for it? Pretend I was lost? Face up to the truth and risk certain arrest? If I went to jail, what would happen to Lawrence?

I heard the sound of footsteps descending the staircase behind me as I stared straight ahead in anticipation of the next command.

"Wait right there," the voice said.

Hightailing it out of there seemed like a bad idea. So did faking I was lost. I was hungry and thirsty and tired of running. I elected to go with the option of dealing with law enforcement face-to-face. Less to think about that way. I turned around to face the combined consequences of twenty-four hours on the lam. "Officer, I can expl—"

He wasn't a police officer. The man walking across the Allen Fieldhouse basketball court looked like a janitor. He carried a push broom and a burlap sack. Still, he had a voice of authority that sounded like the prime minister of janitors. As he got closer, I couldn't help but think I'd seen him somewhere before. For the life of me, I couldn't remember when or where.

The janitor wore round glasses. He was maybe thirty years old and an inch shorter than me. There was the faint hint of a Canadian accent in his voice. His black hair was slicked down and parted in the center. His face was rugged and angular, with strong features, and he had the bushiest mustache I'd ever seen.

"What is your name, young fellow?"

"Ezekiel Archer, sir."

"Where are you from?"

"Los Angeles, sir."

"Sakes alive, lad, you are a long way from home."

Los Angeles was half a country away, but there was something about standing on the Allen Fieldhouse basketball court that felt like home, as if I belonged there.

I felt more at ease now, because the janitor seemed friendly. I had a hunch he wouldn't call security. I noticed a name patch sewn onto his overalls. The janitor's name was James, but that wasn't enough of a clue to help me remember where I'd seen him before.

"The fact is, you are trespassing. No one is allowed onto the court, unless of course you are on the University of Kansas basketball team. I do not remember seeing the last name Archer on Coach Worth's spring practice roster."

Coach Worth was Bob Worth, KU's head basketball coach. I'd met him when he came to Los Angeles on a recruiting trip last year. He attended one of my games early in the season and asked how I'd feel about playing at the college level, where basketball was born. I had two letters at my apartment from Coach Worth. The first one offered me an athletic scholarship to the university. The second rescinded that scholarship because of the melee at the city finals.

"Sorry to have bothered you, sir," I said to the janitor. "I should go."

It was time to find Lawrence and figure out a way to gas up Wade's truck so we could drive to the bus station and wait for Curtis and Stretch. I walked over to where my ball had come to rest under the basket and bent down to pick it up. I must have risen too quickly, because I felt lightheaded. The next thing I knew, I was lying flat on my back on the court. When I opened my eyes, the janitor was towering over me, his thick eyebrows drawn together in an expression of concern.

"You went down like a duck falling off a rock," he said. "Are you all right?"

"I'm fine, just a little hungry, is all."

James reached down and helped me to a sitting position. "Goodness, son, where did you get that handcuff, and what in the world happened to that hand?"

"It's nothing, just a little burn," I said, ignoring the handcuff inquiry and downplaying the severity of my injury.

James rummaged through his burlap sack and pulled out a glass medicine bottle and a roll of gauze. He uncorked the bottle and poured its thick contents onto the palm of my blistered hand, smearing it around until the entire burned area was covered. The salve smelled like someone had doused an angry skunk with a beaker of cheap cologne, but I didn't say anything to James, because I didn't want to offend him.

"Made it myself. I know, it smells awful, but it works."

He wrapped my hand in the gauze and tied the ends together to hold it in place. I felt the pain subside, but that only made my hunger more noticeable. James reached into his burlap sack again, this time emerging with a piece of fruit.

"Peach? I dare say, it is just what the doctor ordered."

I had second thoughts about accepting food from a man who looked like he couldn't afford to give it to me, but my survival instinct kicked in. "Sure, thanks."

I scarfed it down and felt a flood of energy run through my body and the color return to my face. When James seemed to be satisfied that I was strong enough, he set down his burlap sack and extended his arms to help me to my feet. As he pulled me up, I noticed the word NAISMITH stenciled in retro-style letters on his burlap sack.

The arena was located on Naismith Drive, so that probably meant the burlap sack was property of the university. Or maybe it was a souvenir giveaway from Jayhawk Vintage Burlap Sack Night at a recent university sporting event.

"I best be going now," I said. "I've got a long trip home."

"Be safe, Zeke," James said as he waved goodbye, picked up his broom and burlap sack, and walked back up the arena's steps.

I watched James ascend the stairway and disappear into the darkness. I spun my basketball and processed my time spent with the janitor, trying to figure out how all the jigsaw puzzle pieces fit together. I examined the facts:

Naismith.
Canadian accent.
Bushy mustache.
James.
Thick eyebrows.
First aid.
Peach.
Just what the doctor ordered.

Then it hit me like a lightning bolt through the trees. Was the janitor a direct descendent of Dr. James Naismith, inventor of the game of basketball? Of course, it couldn't be the actual Dr. Naismith, because every student of the game knew he had died decades ago.

But hold on, something wasn't right. The janitor had said, "Be safe, *Zeke*." He'd called me Zeke, even though I'd told him my name was Ezekiel. How did he know my nickname?

Like everything else I'd witnessed in the past twenty-four hours, especially what went down with Lawrence at the tree-lined corner of 7th Avenue and Dimension Street, my chance encounter with a man who looked a lot like a young version of the father of basketball was freaking me out.

My hands grew clammy. When would all the weirdness stop and life get back to normal? Would there ever be a normal again without basketball? I wanted to let out a scream, but choked it down for fear of attracting unwanted attention from campus security. I closed my eyes and listened for Wade's voice inside my head, but silence was the only sound.

If Wade were standing next to me, he'd say, *"Allow me to introduce you to each other. Zeke, I'd like you to meet your fear. Fear, this is Zeke. Shake hands, gentlemen."*

Wade used to say those words whenever I panicked over a tough opponent in park league. The way to overcome fear, he told me, was through enlightenment. Learn all you can about your adversary. Ask questions and listen for the answers. Know your rival like you know yourself.

The truth was, I had no idea if Wade were still alive—or lying dead in a military hospital morgue. But I knew he would want me to push for answers, because quitting was not an option.

It felt like the 7th Dimension was trying to tell me something. But without Lawrence around to translate, I had to figure it out on my own.

I summoned my last ounce of courage.

"Dr. James Naismith celebrity lookalike, or whoever the hell you are, show yourself. Now!"

34

There's No Easy Way to Say This

I was so delirious from hunger and lack of sleep that I thought I had finally lost my mind. The ghost of Dr. James Naismith had a one-cameo-appearance maximum, and he'd exited stage left without making a curtain call.

It was time to find Lawrence and make my way to the bus station to wait for Curtis and Stretch to arrive. After I would deliver the news of the Entity's decision to render the sport obsolete, Curtis would be understanding and supportive, while Stretch, the aspiring private eye, would probe deeper and pummel me with questions for which I had no answers.

We'd all wait together at the bus station for the westbound Greyhound to show up. I'd make sure the guys got on it and looked after Lawrence until his father picked him up at the downtown Los Angeles bus terminal. That would allow me a solo drive home so I could figure out a game plan for a new life—one that didn't include fast breaks, crossover dribbles, or high-post pick and rolls.

I'd taken a couple of steps toward the exit when the now-familiar otherworldly voice shook me to the core.

"'Show yourself,' eh? Goodness, where are your manners, Ezekiel? Could you not at least say *please*?"

I saw the shadowy figure of the janitor looming at the upper reaches of the arena.

"Yes, sir. Sorry, sir."

"Seems it is often about confrontation with you, young man."

Not only did the janitor understand the finer points of nutritional science and burn therapy, but he also had a firm grasp of the concept of conflict resolution. He walked down the stairs and across the basketball court until he stood before me. I felt my knees tremble when he motioned for me to hand over my ball. The janitor bounced it on the hardwood a few times as if to gauge its game worthiness.

"I must say, Chip once carried a sterling line of basketball gear," he said.

Once carried? Apparently, news of an errant meteorite crashing into the basketball equipment section of Chip's Sporting Goods had made it all the way to eastern Kansas. The janitor returned my ball with a well-executed chest-high bounce pass.

It was time to reexamine my options. The way I saw it, there were only two. I could make a graceful exit, or I could stand my ground and ask the obvious question. I chose the latter.

"Who are you?"

"Fair question, Ezekiel. Who do you think I am?"

Well played, sir. The janitor had pulled a Ruby-in-Denver by answering my question with an excellent one of his own.

"I don't believe you're the janitor, and I don't think you're Dr. James Naismith, because he's dead, and besides, I've seen pictures. You look a lot younger than he did when he died, which was a really long time ago."

"November twenty-eight, 1939, to be precise."

I established that the janitor was a sports history buff, but he still hadn't answered my question. I was exhausted and scared. I felt beads of sweat rolling down my forehead. With the game of basketball possibly no longer in the equation, I had a lot less to live for, so I went for it.

"With all due respect, sir, how about you just cut the crap and tell me who the hell you are?"

"Dear boy, I am trying to ease you into it."

"Please just tell me. It's late and I need to get going. I've got friends relying on me."

"Yes, I know. It was like that for you in the recent past, friends relying on you, and you let them down."

"Sir?"

James changed the subject. "The Greyhound bus from Los Angeles will arrive at the Lawrence bus station at eight fifty-five a.m., as scheduled."

That was downright weird and creepy. I had never mentioned anything about Curtis and Stretch coming in on the bus. Not that it mattered, since there was no longer a tournament.

"Mister, tell me who you are and why you're here."

"Your ability to perceive the truth about who I am and why I stand before you may be limited by what you already know to be true."

I let that statement marinate in my skull, but it only left me more confused. "I don't think I—"

"I will tell you, but if I do, your life will never be the same. It is your decision."

Decision making hadn't been my best attribute lately, starting with the high school finals. Lawrence would soon panic over why I was loitering in the arena for so long. Curtis and Stretch would soon step off the bus wondering why the greeting committee wasn't there.

"You need to take it on faith that I can handle whatever it is you're so reluctant to tell me."

The man studied my face as if to measure my worthiness to receive the burden of his truth. As he did, I searched his eyes for a sign as to why our paths had crossed. I thought I saw the sum total of my life standing at the free-throw line at the front end of a one-and-one, the kind of moment where you must clear the hurdle in your path in order to move forward.

"All right, Ezekiel, as you wish. The truth is, I stand before you as a representative of the 7th Dimension."

Check, please.

"There is more. Earth exists under the unifying principle that, while all life-forms vibrate at unique levels of interactivity, they are connected in a cosmic interdimensional reality."

I felt the wisp of a cool breeze flowing between my ears. I knew that words were coming out of James's mouth, because I saw his lips moving, but I had no idea what he had just said. I began to spin the ball on my fingertip reflexively. He must have sensed my confusion.

"Perhaps it is best if I put this into terms you can better understand," he said. "Basically, the planet is like one big, never-ending basketball tournament. Every team is invited to play, the rules are infinite, and no two team uniforms are alike."

"Let's pretend for a moment I understood that," I said, knowing I was in over my head. I had doubts about the wisdom of asking the obvious follow-up question, but I was in too deep to stop. "How does the 7th Dimension fit in?"

"The Entity known as the 7th Dimension was created at a universal life-force distribution center located in a distant galaxy," James said. "The Entity hitched a ride on the tail of a comet that traveled through a paranormal vortex and slammed into Earth three hundred and seventy-five million years ago. Made quite a splash, literally," he said with a chuckle. "The 7th Dimension landed in the middle of what is now the Pacific Ocean."

James explained that the 7th Dimension's first order of business was to seed Earth's landmasses over the next five million years. Once trees appeared on dry land, the Entity reestablished itself in the intertwined root systems of those trees, where it lives today as a singular energy being using the planet's three trillion trees as antennas for its communications network.

"It is a little-known fact that the 7th Dimension had the idea for trees to produce oxygen," the janitor said. "A no-brainer, one of the Entity's best, and it set the stage for the arrival of your ancient relatives."

James told me that humans' earliest ancestors first appeared on Earth six million years ago. He said the 7th Dimension had been there from the beginning, guiding the different levels of humanity through the development of a higher consciousness over thousands of centuries. The Entity's presence and encouragement, he said, had enabled humankind to evolve into the modern civilization of today.

But there was a problem.

"The Entity discovered that humankind's DNA has tiny errors embedded in the programming that sometimes cause humans to perform evil acts, so the 7th Dimension looked for ways to counterbalance that type of behavior. Most recently, this had taken the form of the invention of basketball."

The janitor had finally connected the dots.

"In 1890, the 7th Dimension set the wheels of invention into motion when it caught wind of a young Canadian fellow who had the exact character and credentials it needed." James described the man as a physical education instructor, a Presbyterian minister, and a future doctor of medicine.

"Here is where this gets even more difficult for you, Ezekiel."

Not possible.

"Your suspicions were correct. I am Dr. James Naismith, inventor of the game of basketball. But there is more."

There always is.

"I am not the James Naismith from the 1930s you have seen pictures of in your sports history books. I am the James Naismith of December twenty-first, 1891, the day the first basketball game was played."

"Sir?"

"The Entity serves as my travel agent whenever it requires that I represent it in important basketball affairs—like this one."

The ball wobbled off my index finger and landed on top of my foot, propelling it along the court toward Dr. Naismith. In one motion, he flipped it up with his shoe, caught it, and spun it on his own index finger as he continued.

"Now you know who I am. You also asked why I am here."

I no longer wanted to know. I had a gut feeling it wouldn't be good news, but it was clear that the 1891 version of Dr. Naismith had a job to do.

"There is no easy way to say this. The Entity arranged for us to meet at Allen Fieldhouse so I could explain to you, in person, why you caused the game of basketball to be taken away from humankind."

That was the point in time when I would normally say "*Ballgame*," but I couldn't get the word out, because my heart was stuck in my throat.

35

There's Something Else I Need to Tell You Before I Go

Dr. James Naismith, formerly known as the janitor, sent my basketball back to me with a zippy two-hand chest pass. It was a textbook toss but a pointless gesture, since my ball would be of little use once I left Allen Fieldhouse for the first and last time.

However, I do some of my best thinking with a basketball in my hands. When I caught the ball, an idea popped into my head.

"I don't suppose we could play a game of horse for the chance to reverse the Entity's decision?"

"Goodness, no. I am afraid that will not be possible."

Dr. Naismith's rejection of my proposition was reminiscent of the manner in which Stretch had tomahawked Brock's shot in the three-on-three finals at Jefferson. With no possibility of saving the game, there was nothing left to do but head for the bus station for a conversation I wasn't looking forward to having with Curtis and Stretch. I took the high road with Dr. Naismith as I made my exit.

"It was a pleasure to meet you, sir. I understand my actions at the city finals were the reason behind the 7th Dimension's decision. I was hoping the Entity would reconsider, but I take full responsibility."

I reached out to shake Dr. Naismith's hand with my bandaged and handcuffed one. He met my palm with a firm grasp and hung onto it longer than I expected.

"I do not get out much these days, so I am not in a big hurry to get back," said Dr. Naismith with a twinkle in his eye. "I believe you have a few hours before the bus carrying your friends arrives. Would you like to learn a little more about the origins of the game? You might find it useful for your future."

"I don't want to get into trouble for being in the arena any longer than I already have been."

"I believe that will not be a problem."

I didn't say anything to Dr. Naismith, but I was worried about Lawrence. He had been alone upstairs for a long time now. I didn't want him to freak out—or worse, to walk back to Los Angeles. Dr. Naismith seemed to sense my concern.

"Your friend has been keeping busy. You need not worry about him."

I knew the opportunity was a fleeting one, so I sat down on the court and braced myself for the unknown.

Dr. Naismith explained that early in his life, he set a goal to educate, train, and mentor young men and women. That's when he first caught the attention of the 7th Dimension. In the fall of 1890, he traveled to the YMCA's training school in Springfield, Massachusetts, where he met Dr. Luther Gulick, the dean of the school's Physical Education Department.

"Cold winter weather forced students indoors to get their exercise," Dr. Naismith said. "Football proved to be too rough. The young folks swiftly became bored with calisthenics and gymnastics. In November of 1891, Dr. Gulick challenged me to come up with a game that would maintain student interest while reducing the risk of injury."

Dr. Naismith explained that he wanted to incorporate elements of physical conditioning, strength, agility, teamwork, fairness, grace, and integrity into the new game. He said trial and error with variations of football, soccer, rugby, and lacrosse led to instructional opportunities in the application of first aid, but nothing more.

Hope was fading that he could meet Dr. Gulick's mandate, but in a moment of inspiration, Dr. Naismith drew from his own childhood experiences and developed the basic framework of what was initially known as Basket Ball.

"At that point, I needed to mount two goals in the gymnasium, so I asked the YMCA's building superintendent if he had any wooden boxes that were eighteen inches square. He did not, but instead he offered me two peach baskets he was keeping in storage."

Dr. Naismith said he nailed the peach baskets onto the ten-foot-high railing at either end of the gym's gallery. After that, he sat down at his desk with a pencil and drafted basketball's original thirteen rules.

"Most of the rules covered the fundamentals of the new game," Dr. Naismith said. "If I had to choose the single most important rule, I would say it was number five, the one that disqualifies a player for the rest of the game if he exhibits evident intent to injure another person."

Dr. Naismith stared long and hard at me after delivering those words. He didn't need to explain further, but he chose to anyway.

"I included rule number five, because I wanted my students to consider the basic philosophy that violence as a means of resolving conflict does not work. Of course, it is a concept that transcends basketball, but basketball seemed at the time like a constructive place for it to take root."

Dr. Naismith told me he moved to Denver in 1895 to take a job at the local YMCA and attend medical school. After he received his doctor of medicine degree in 1898, the University of Kansas recruited him to be head of the Physical Education Department, a position that included the responsibility of chapel director. Once on campus at KU, he said he took the initiative to introduce and promote his new game. Dr. Naismith served as basketball coach, professor, physician, and athletic director over a forty-year span, interrupted only by a stint as a military chaplain during World War I.

Even though Dr. Naismith invented basketball at the Springfield YMCA, I knew that many fans considered the University of Kansas to be the birthplace of the game. I asked him for clarification.

"I was never too concerned about where it all started, only that the game accomplish its intended purpose," Dr. Naismith said. "I was working at KU when basketball first gained popularity, so it was logical for folks to think I invented it there. That said, I have always credited the YMCA for basketball's widespread international appeal."

Dr. Naismith offered to change the dressing on my injured hand. I accepted, even if it meant my hand would not smell better anytime soon. He cleaned the wound and reapplied his homemade salve before wrapping it in fresh gauze. My hand felt better, but that was small consolation compared to the feeling of loss that lingered from the finality of the Entity's decision.

"How are you doing, time-wise?" Dr. Naismith said.

I hadn't looked at my watch since missing the Entity's midnight deadline, so I was surprised to find out it was well after two o'clock in the morning. "I'm good. Why?"

"We might not have the opportunity to compare notes like this again, so there are a few more things I want you to know before I leave."

It was hard to imagine feeling worse than I already did, so I thought I could handle whatever the inventor of the game threw at me. "Sure, fire away."

"Throughout the history of humankind, the 7th Dimension has recognized and honored great leaders by working behind the scenes to place them in positions of guardianship within their communities. Early evidence of this can be traced back ten thousand years to the Neolithic age in China through cliff carvings and pictographs made by early human agricultural communities."

As Dr. Naismith cited other examples of the Entity's influence in fostering guardianship over the centuries, I wondered where it was going. "I suppose there's a connection to basketball in there somewhere?"

"As a matter of fact, there is," he said. "It is a little-known fact that the world's first wheel, invented in approximately five thousand BC, was a precursor to the modern-day basketball." Dr. Naismith had a glint in his eye on that one. "Once the game had found its footing in the early twentieth century, the 7th Dimension sought to ensure basketball's survival by granting to a small group of people the privilege of safeguarding its existence and promoting its values."

Dr. Naismith told me that the first person the Entity chose was Phog Allen, who came to be known as the "father of basketball coaching."

"Then there was Meadowlark Lemon, the Clown Prince of the Harlem Globetrotters. Goodness, could he handle the basketball."

I knew about the Harlem Globetrotters, because my dad took me to see them perform during my first season of park league basketball. The Globetrotters are an exhibition team that combines court skills with comedy to entertain basketball fans around the globe. Meadowlark Lemon was the team's leader for more than two decades. Many players have credited him as an important influence in their careers.

"Then there is young Jason McElwain, one of the Entity's top selections, in my humble opinion," Dr. Naismith said.

Dr. Naismith told me that Jason, a high-functioning autistic student-athlete from Greece Athena High School in New

York, had served as his varsity basketball team's manager. Head coach Jim Johnson added Jason to the roster in a game against rival Spencerport High so he could earn a team jersey and sit on the bench for Greece Athena's final home game.

What followed was something Dr. Naismith described as "utterly amazing." He said Coach Johnson inserted Jason into the game with a little more than four minutes to play and a comfortable lead. "Jason missed his first couple of shots, then got 'hot as a pistol,' as Jason himself said during a postgame interview, making six long-range three-pointers and a two-ball, finishing with twenty points. His performance continues to serve as an inspiration to those battling adversity."

Dr. Naismith named other players and coaches the Entity had chosen for guardianship, people such as John Wooden, "Pistol Pete" Maravich, Kareem Abdul-Jabbar, Lisa Leslie, Yao Ming, Nancy Lieberman, Becky Hammon, and Magic Johnson.

"There is one more thing I need to tell you before I go," he said. "The Entity had already chosen its next guardian of the game just hours before its decision to take basketball away."

I gazed downward to avoid making eye contact with Dr. Naismith.

"The game's next guardian was you, Zeke."

I closed my eyes to process what Dr. Naismith had told me. When I did, tears rolled down my cheeks.

36

This Was Never Really About Basketball

Just when I thought it was not possible to feel any worse, Dr. Naismith's devastating revelation proved me wrong. The pained look on his face told me how difficult it was to deliver that news. "I am truly sorry, Ezekiel."

I always knew I had a deep and intimate connection to the game. But the next guardian of the game?

"Why me?"

"As I understand it, the Entity was struck by your commitment to the principles of basketball, in particular the elements of fairness, grace, and integrity. You understand the importance of nurturing your physical body, so conditioning, strength, and agility come naturally to you. Wade taught you everything you needed to know about teamwork through his words and actions."

Dr. Naismith knew my brother? That caught me off guard.

"You've met Wade?"

"In a manner of speaking."

Dr. Naismith said that in order for the Entity to select the most qualified guardians, it had to be deeply familiar with the talent pool. That meant knowing every person on the planet. "In a sense, you cannot tell the players without a scorecard," Dr. Naismith said.

Dr. Naismith told me the 7th Dimension involved him in personnel matters relating to basketball, so he'd studied my brother's actions over the years as he assessed my guardianship qualifications.

I had no idea if Wade was all right. Asking Dr. Naismith if he knew Wade's status was a real long shot, but I asked anyway. "In case you didn't know, Wade was shot while on a peacekeeping mission in Afghanistan. He underwent surgery at a military hospital in Germany. Do you know if he's okay?"

Dr. Naismith wrinkled his forehead and squinted as if looking inward. "All I can tell you is that your brother is on the ultimate journey."

The finality of Dr. Naismith's words sent a shockwave of sadness through my body and caused me to lose track of what we were talking about before the conversation shifted to Wade.

"Teamwork," Dr. Naismith said.

"Huh?"

"It is what Wade taught you through words and actions," he said, "like the time he helped coach your park league team when you were just starting out. Or the way he encouraged you to trust and nurture your friendship with Curtis and Stretch. Or the single most heroic example of teamwork, joining the corps and putting the welfare of his fellow marines before his own, at the risk of his own life."

That left fairness, grace, and integrity. Dr. Naismith told me the 7th Dimension had taken note of the evenhanded way I combined elements of all three, on and off the basketball court.

"The 7th Dimension timed your future guardianship to coincide with troubling events in the game's recent history," he said. "The Entity witnessed basketball's intended purpose begin to erode because of violence, greed, and corruption. It felt you had the inner strength to stem the tide, or even reverse the trend altogether."

Dr. Naismith explained that the 7th Dimension was so stunned by the violence at the city finals that it brought him back in for consultation. He said the session had taken place in a conference room that circled the globe.

"Frankly, I was surprised to get the call," he said. "We had already voted you in unanimously. It was a done deal."

I felt a wave of nausea and my chin quiver as I bore the weight of the responsibility for causing such a high-level conference to take place. Dr. Naismith said the Entity felt the game of basketball had run its course and could no longer achieve its intended purpose.

"The 7th Dimension thought that if basketball had degenerated so badly that guardian-in-training Zeke Archer, in the biggest game of his life, could send a referee to the emergency room, then there was simply no hope left. It was time to abandon the game and get back to the drawing board."

Dr. Naismith told me that the Entity had studied my reaction to the impending decision to eliminate the game as it looked for new ways to carry out its mandate on Earth.

But something didn't sound right.

"My reaction was based on Lawrence's ability to pick up 7th Dimension radio signals," I said. "I suppose you're going to tell me the Entity arranged for that too?"

Dr. Naismith chuckled and smiled. "Smart lad, that Lawrence. The Entity did not see it coming. I am not sure it is possible for an interdimensional energy being to be caught off guard, but news of Lawrence interconnecting seven pencils heptagonally to intercept communiqués was met with bemused head scratching in the Entity boardroom."

Dr. Naismith said rather than deny Lawrence a skill achieved through ingenuity and perseverance, the Entity had allowed him to use his gift as a way to honor both Lawrence and the Entity's cause.

"What about when the 7th Dimension warned Lawrence never to speak with me about its plans?"

"Pure gamesmanship on the part of the Entity," Dr. Naismith said. "It knows that when people are asked to do something but not given an adequate reason for the request, their reaction is often the opposite of the one requested."

From that point forward, according to Dr. Naismith, the 7th Dimension set up obstacles and gauged my reaction to them, all in preparation for our chance encounter at Allen Fieldhouse.

"The 7th Dimension worked through Lawrence to create a bridge world that would bring you here, so I could explain everything."

With a hopeless sense of loss looming and nothing left to do but make the long drive home, I was anxious for Dr. Naismith to wrap up the Entity's business, so I could get on with my life.

"Start explaining."

"I do not blame you for your impatience," Dr. Naismith said. "I felt the same way in 1891 as I was inventing basketball and the incorrigible hooligans in my class only wanted to tackle each other in the gymnasium."

Dr. Naismith said the first obstacles the 7th Dimension put into motion were the most symbolic: taking down the rims and nets from the court at the rec center, followed by removing my basketball from the apartment. Then the Entity upped the ante by staging a burglary at Chip's Sporting Goods before hurtling a real-life meteorite through the roof and into the basketball equipment section.

"Chip's delightful store was collateral damage, unfortunately," Dr. Naismith said. "I was against that decision but was overruled by majority vote."

"I suppose you're going to tell me Lawrence really didn't win $7,777,777 at World Famous Calvin's?"

"Oh, that slot machine jackpot was real, all right. And even though you two were not old enough to gamble, the Entity arranged for the real Calvin to pay it out. That was an integrity test. You passed."

I asked Dr. Naismith about our encounters with law enforcement agencies in three states. He told me the 7th Dimension feared for our safety by the time we got to eastern Utah on no sleep and little food, so it sent in one of its top operatives, State Trooper Chance Hunter, to put a stop to the road trip.

But in a rare mix-up, the Entity was conducting a concurrent basketball gear removal operation at Utah Basketball Equipment Company, and Trooper Hunter made an on-the-spot decision to go after the bigger criminal fish.

"So much had happened to you by the time you made it to Denver, the 7th Dimension felt it was only fair to create an opportunity for you to visit your father. That is when it tinkered with the Chevy's carburetor and dispatched a Colorado State Patrol cruiser to assist you and ensure your safety."

When the truck broke down on I-70 in Denver, I'd felt curious about why State Trooper 777 all but gave me a police escort to my dad's house.

Now that the Colorado law enforcement mystery was solved, that left the ultra-high-speed chase by the Kansas Highway Patrol. I asked Dr. Naismith why the Entity had sat idle while we drove Wade's antique pickup truck in excess of 130 miles per hour to avoid arrest. Wasn't that a bit risky?

"The Entity had nothing to do with that one," Dr. Naismith said.

"Excuse me?" I scratched my jaw with my good hand and went as pale as a ghost.

"No mystery there, just an officer of the law doing his best to protect and serve."

Dr. Naismith said the 7th Dimension was relieved when the Kansas State Trooper erred on the side of caution and threw in the towel. But as hard as we'd tried to beat the deadline, it had never mattered, because the Entity, Dr. Naismith said, had no intention of changing its mind.

"I am afraid this conversation has come full circle," Dr. Naismith said.

"That's it? Basketball is gone forever?"

"Zeke, this was never really about basketball. For three hundred and seventy-five million years, the 7th Dimension has tested the worthiness of those it chose to serve as guardians of the institutions it has held sacred. There is nothing more I can do."

The effects of more than forty-eight hours with no sleep and meager food were setting in. My head throbbed and my mouth felt parched. The Allen Fieldhouse arena spun around like a top as I struggled to hold it together. My shooting hand stung from the severe burn I'd sustained hours earlier. Not that I had much use for a hand that shot a basketball anyway. Those days were long gone.

"I have enjoyed our brief time together, but it is time for me to go," Dr. Naismith said.

I had no strength left in my body and felt like I would pass out. I closed my eyes for a moment and saw an image of Wade floating in my mind. He reached down and placed his hand on my shoulder. I felt a surge of electricity run through me as he spoke:

"There's nothing left to do but sacrifice yourself, marine. It is the only way."

Then Wade drifted off into the clouds and was gone. I opened my eyes and saw Dr. Naismith gathering his burlap sack.

"Wait, I have an idea!" I said as I fell backward onto the court.

"Dear boy, are you all right?"

"Take me!"

"I cannot take you with me."

"No, I mean tell the 7th Dimension to take away my ability to play basketball," I said. "I want to give it up so others can continue to play. You must convince the Entity. It is the only way."

"Zeke, I wish I—"

"Take me!"

My head bounced off the hardwood. I knew it, because I heard the thud. Then the arena went black.

37

Let's Just Do What We Do and Go Home

I blinked and opened my eyes to the sight of a hideous figure hulking over me.

"Man, what's that horrific smell?" Stretch said.

I had no idea where I was. I took a quick look around and found that I was sprawled on a slab of concrete high above some mystery basketball arena. I shook my head and came to my senses. I was in Allen Fieldhouse. I was groggy and there were dozens of players shooting around on the basketball courts below.

"Hope you had a nice nap, sleepyhead," Stretch said. "By the way, you really stink."

That smell wasn't so much me as it was my hand, which was still wrapped in the gauze and ointment applied by the janitor—I mean, Dr. Naismith. Everything was coming back to me.

"Dude, what happened to your hand, and why does it smell like that?" Curtis said.

"Nothing. Burned it. Long story." It was great to see my friends again. I was relieved they'd both made it safely to Allen Fieldhouse.

"Let me help you with that, bro," Curtis said as he unwrapped the bandage. My hand smelled horrible, but it was healed. Not a mark on it. Add another one to the weird column.

"I'm guessing you wrapped your hand in that bandage to conceal the fact that *there's a handcuff on your wrist!*" Stretch said.

"Yeah, long story there too," I said. Curtis and Stretch didn't know the half of it.

"Can you shoot with that thing strapped to your wrist?" Curtis said.

"Not to worry," Stretch said, brandishing a hairpin. "I got this."

"Dude, you carry a bobby pin in your gym bag?" Curtis said.

"It's the life of a private eye," Stretch said as he straightened out the pin and wriggled it into the bracelet's keyway.

Click.

"Remind me to keep you away from my gym locker," Curtis said.

The clock on the scoreboard said 9:30. The western regional three-on-three tournament would start in thirty minutes. If the event was about to get underway, that meant the

Entity hadn't taken away the game after all. What a huge relief. I looked around for Lawrence but couldn't find him.

"Dude, you ever gonna tell us why you ditched us and drove here instead?" Curtis said. "And when did you get your driver's license?"

I ignored his questions and asked one of my own. "How did you guys get to the arena?"

"Imagine our surprise after ridin' the dog for a day and a half when that nerdy kid Lawrence was waiting for us at the bus station in Wade's old jalopy," Stretch said.

Stretch told me he'd called his dad from a pay phone when the Greyhound stopped at the bus terminal in Denver. "Dad said your mom called him in a panic looking for you, something about Chett Biffmann and a busted padlock at a storage unit. Know anything about that?"

Yeah, I knew plenty. "Where's Lawrence?" I asked, ignoring Stretch's question.

"Up there, top row," Curtis said, pointing toward the arena's rafters.

There he was, sitting all alone in the last row. I waved, but Lawrence didn't respond. No worries, I was used to that. I started climbing the steps in his direction.

"Hello? The tournament?" Stretch said. "We need to hit the court."

"You guys head down and warm up," I said. "I'll be there in a couple minutes."

Curtis and Stretch picked up their gear as I made my way to the section of the arena where the air was thin. When I got to the top, I found Lawrence sitting on a concrete bench, arms folded, pencils interconnected in the now-familiar seven-sided configuration on the ground next to my duffel bag.

"I suppose the reception is better up here," I said. No response, so I pressed on. "I'm guessing you got help to gas up the truck and swung by the bus station to pick up the guys while I slept?" Still nothing.

With the tournament about to get underway, it was clear the 7th Dimension had decided to spare the game. That was a relief, but something felt different about basketball, and I couldn't put my finger on it.

"Are you going to tell me what happened?"

Lawrence shook his head to indicate the answer was no. I was running out of time. "Perhaps you can write it down. I've got to get down there. The tournament's about to start."

Lawrence stared off into the distance at nothing in particular as I jogged down the long stairway. When I got halfway to the court, I turned around and saw that he was writing. Maybe I would get some answers, but first there was the business of basketball. The Allen Fieldhouse maintenance crew had transformed the arena from the single basketball court where I met with Dr. Naismith to eight separate half-courts for the tournament, similar to how Coach Kincaid had set up the gym at Jefferson two weeks earlier.

"I checked the schedule," said Curtis, already in uniform and warmed up. "We're up first, at ten. Better get ready, dude."

It was better that way, less time to think about how far in over our heads we were, competing against some of the top high school players in the country. I handed Curtis my basketball and hauled butt to the locker room to change into the vintage silks Mr. Shields had given us. When I came out, Curtis was flexing the ankle he'd sprained at the tournament in Los Angeles.

"How is it?" I asked.

"I'm good, bro," Curtis said. I could tell his ankle wasn't one hundred percent, but I also knew there was no way it would affect his ability to shoot or his will to compete.

Stretch was loosening up near the registration table. When he stood up straight, he seemed taller than usual.

"I checked us in already," he said. "I asked the medical staff to measure me. Seems I grew another inch on the bus. Must have been the food. I'm six eleven."

"I thought you looked geekier than usual," I said. "Guess I was right."

Stretch's overnight growth spurt came as encouraging news, because we needed every advantage against players who were more rested than we were. As in the three-on-three event at Jefferson, there were thirty-two teams, and the tournament was single elimination. That meant it was win or drive home. The scoring rules were the same too.

A man standing at center court picked up a microphone to address the crowd. "Good morning," he said, his voice booming over the arena's loudspeakers. "I'm Bob Worth, head coach here at the University of Kansas. Welcome to the annual Jayhawk western regional three-on-three basketball tournament."

Coach Worth didn't need to introduce himself, because every person in the state of Kansas, basketball fan or not, knew who he was. Players gathered into groups of three as Coach Worth went over the tournament rules. Maybe it was a coach thing, but he spent extra time reviewing the details of my favorite rule.

"Good sportsmanship is key, gentlemen," Coach Worth said. "Let's remember that today." By that point in my life, rule number five was woven into every fabric of my being. Forgetting it would be like forgetting the sun would come up in the morning.

"The winner of today's tournament will compete for the national title this fall," Coach Worth said, "and you'll be pleased to know we'll host it right here at Allen Fieldhouse." That announcement brought a round of applause from players and their family and friends who were scattered around the arena.

News of a subsequent national tournament was comforting, because it meant the game would be around after the western regional event ended. I waved the guys over for a pregame strategy session near the court where we would face our first opponent, a team representing the City of Brotherly Love, Philadelphia.

"We got a scouting report on these dudes?" Curtis said.

"I watched them warm up," Stretch said. "They're strong and athletic."

"Listen up," I said before telling the guys we needed to keep it simple and stick with the fundamentals. I looked directly into Stretch's eyes and reached skyward to poke him in the chest for maximum emphasis. "Patrol the boards and force the ball to the outside. On offense, hang out in the low post. We'll find you."

"Piece of cake," he said.

I put my hands on Curtis's shoulders and delivered his part

of the game plan. He was familiar with it, because it never changed. "Draw your guy out onto the perimeter. That'll open up the interior for Stretch and me to run the pick and roll. Last thing: Remember, you're Curtis Short, human scoring machine. Take every shot you get."

The ref blew his whistle, we shook hands with our opponents, and we won the coin toss. Somehow, after all we'd been through to make it that far, things were looking up.

"Let's just do what we do and go home," were my final instructions.

It must have worked, because we throttled the trio from Philadelphia before beating squads from New York, Chicago, and Bloomington, Indiana.

Curtis's ankle throbbed throughout all four games, but his torrid shooting masked the pain. Stretch was pummeled with elbows but never backed off, swatting shots on defense and dropping in skyhooks whenever he got the ball in deep. I fought through fatigue and dehydration, running the floor and setting the table for the guys.

Somehow we made it to the finals. News of our success blared over the arena's PA system. "Congratulations to the team from McDerney Continuation in Los Angeles," the public address announcer said. "McDerney will play for the tournament championship against a group of young fellas from our very own Lawrence, Kansas."

The guys and I sat together on a bench, toweling off sweat and pondering our fate, unlikely participants in what was about to be the biggest basketball game of our lives.

38

We've Got These Guys on the Run

I scanned the arena and took stock of the crowd. It didn't look as though any of the other thirty teams or their supporters had left the building. Everyone settled into the premium seats, the ones that were surely the most prized whenever the University of Kansas basketball team took the court.

The arena's horn sounded, bringing down the noise level in Allen Fieldhouse to a quiet buzz. I huddled with the guys as the announcer made the introductions. "Please join me in welcoming the team from McDerney. Give a warm Kansas round of applause to Curtis Short, Roland Puckett, and team captain Ezekiel Archer."

The applause was polite but sparse. I sensed that everyone would be pulling for the home team. Our opponents were our age, but they carried themselves like college seniors as they stood across the court dressed in royal blue and crimson red, with the team's name embroidered onto the front of their jerseys.

The announcer continued: "Please welcome, all the way from Lawrence, Kansas, the Future Jayhawks! These future freshmen will play basketball right here at the University of Kansas this fall. Please put your hands together for Jack Diamond, Tripp Wheeler, and team captain Colton Banner!"

Cue the thunderous applause.

"Good luck today, gentlemen!" were the announcer's final words of introduction.

I had a feeling we would need a lot more than luck to beat those guys. One of the two referees blew his whistle and motioned for both teams to join him at center court. When we got there, Colton Banner approached me with an outstretched hand.

"Hey, Zeke, we heard about what happened back in Los Angeles," he said. "Sorry things didn't work out. The guys and I were looking forward to playing with you this season."

I recalled Coach Worth saying something about Colton Banner and his teammates during the coach's recruiting trip to Los Angeles the year before. Coach Worth must have mentioned my name to them, because Colton Banner knew exactly who I was.

"Thanks, man," was all I said in response. There wasn't much else to say.

The referees covered the ground rules. I won't mention whether they went into great detail about rule number you-know-what because the answer was obvious. We stood for the coin flip. The Future Jayhawks won the right to call heads or tails because they'd beaten their four previous opponents by more combined points than we had.

The referee placed a shiny silver dollar on top of his thumb and issued his instructions. "Call it in the air." He flipped the coin as Colton Banner called heads. When I tracked the flight of the coin as it tumbled end-over-end, something else bright and shiny caught my attention halfway up the arena. I shifted my focus and squinted. The glistening object was a cluster of metal campaign ribbons pinned to an olive-green military uniform worn by a man standing on crutches at the concourse entrance to the arena. I rubbed my eyes.

"Heads, it is," the referee said.

The man wearing that uniform smiled and saluted me.

It was Wade.

He was alive.

I burst into tears, right there at center court.

"Buck up, kid, it's only the coin toss," Stretch said.

I was a total mess. I'd never felt so relieved in my life. I wanted to run into the stands to give my big brother a hug and tell him everything that had happened over the past couple of weeks.

"Ball out to the Future Jayhawks," the referee said.

Curtis seemed to know something was out of kilter. "What's up, bro?"

I thought about telling Curtis that Wade was in the house, but I didn't want to burden him with anything beyond the immediate task at hand, which was trying to hang on against an opponent that everyone in the building wanted to win the title.

"It's nothing," I said. "I'm good. Let's do this."

The first team to twenty points would be crowned the western regional champion, and there was no win-by-two rule. The Future Jayhawks wasted little time in exerting their influence as Colton Banner caught the inbounds pass, put me in the popcorn machine with a razor-sharp head fake, and dropped in an eighteen-footer from the wing.

It was 1–0, Future Jayhawks. Ball out to McDerney.

I inbounded the basketball to Stretch at the high post and set a pick on Curtis's man while Curtis cut for open space. Stretch hit him in stride, and the best sharpshooter west of the Rockies decided to go in for a layup. Curtis banked home the shot to tie the score, but he came down on his defender's foot.

Crack!

The crowd gasped in horror.

Curtis rolled his ankle—his good ankle—and dropped to the deck in a heap.

The referee blew his whistle. "Officials' timeout."

Stretch and I helped Curtis to his feet. He tried to put weight on his ankle but collapsed because the pain was too great. We helped him back up again.

"How is it?" I asked, fearing Curtis would tell me the truth.

"Just a scratch, dude," he said, fighting back tears. "Nineteen more of those and we can go home."

Curtis didn't want to take off his shoe for fear of what he might find, and no amount of rubbing it with dirt—if there even had been any dirt to rub with—would make the swelling go down.

One of the refs came over to assess Curtis's medical condition. "How do you feel, son? Can you play on it?"

"Yeah, I'm good." That was far less than the truth, but none of us had traveled all the way to eastern Kansas to give up because of a debilitating injury.

The referees motioned Colton Banner and me over for a conference. They said I had five minutes to decide whether Curtis could continue. The rules did not allow us to compete with only two players. If Curtis was unable to go, the Future Jayhawks would win the western regional title—by forfeit.

"That's not going to happen," Curtis said when we told him our dilemma. "You dudes remember the game against Rolling Valley?"

Hard to forget that one. It was the opening round of the tournament at Jefferson. We were down 7–zip before Curtis conducted a seminar in the art of shooting a basketball, drilling ten in a row from downtown. If there were any chance of taking the western regional title, Curtis would have to plant himself beyond the arc on offense while Stretch and I covered Colton Banner and his teammates on defense.

"What do you say, son? Can you play?" the ref asked.

Curtis said he could.

"Ball out to the Future Jayhawks."

Colton Banner, who was bigger and stronger than me, demonstrated why he was the number-one high school recruit in the nation, hitting three more midrange jumpers in rapid succession that put us in a 4–1 hole.

On our next possession, Curtis and I worked the ball back and forth until Stretch found room in the low post. When I got it to him, he turned for a skyhook as Jack Diamond and Tripp Wheeler dropped down to double-team him. When Stretch went up for the shot, Jack Diamond leaped high to try and block it while Tripp Wheeler steadied himself near the rim to draw the offensive foul. Stretch got scissored and fell hard to the hardwood in a mass of skinny limbs. The shot rimmed out, the referee blew his whistle, and my blood did a swift boil.

"Foul!"

There once was a time when, without thinking it all the way through, I would have gone after those two players for hurting my best friend. I guess you could say I was older and wiser now from the events that had followed my actions at the city finals. Curtis hobbled over to help me right the big man, who unfolded from the floor in sections.

"Anybody get the license number of that truck?" That was Stretch's way of letting us know he was all right, but when he air-balled both free throws, I knew he was playing hurt. And with Curtis anchored to the court and unable to do much more than cast away from ultra-long range, we were in big trouble.

For the first time in my basketball career, I had no idea how to get us out of a tough jam. Winning was no longer the priority. Instead, I needed to find a way to keep us from getting embarrassed. I glanced up to the concourse entrance for any kind of moral support from Wade, but he wasn't there. I wondered whether I'd really seen him before or if it had just been more 7th Dimension trickery.

Colton Banner hit three more shots to extend his team's lead to 7–1. We were getting slaughtered. I wasn't sure we'd ever score again. It was worse than sitting in detention with Brock and Mrs. Vanderhorst.

Then a familiar voice said something I hadn't heard in years. "Time to take the team on your back, Zeke."

The arena was noisy, but there was no mistaking that voice. Wade had worked his way down to the floor level. I spotted him a few rows up on the opposite side of the court, his crutches sprawled across the seat in front of him.

"You're all out of options," Wade said. "It's all you." Wade used to say that to me in park league when a game was on the line and I was my team's best and sometimes only hope.

From that moment forward, I took over the game.

I finally figured out I was a half step quicker than Colton Banner, and that was the advantage I needed to turn the game around. On offense, I went after him by taking the ball hard to the hole, or dishing it off to Curtis for a wide-open shot from outside the three-point line, or lobbing it in to Stretch for an easy dunk. On defense, I crawled inside Colton Banner's jersey and never left.

We clawed our way back into it on nothing more than sheer will and high-percentage shooting. When I dropped in a runner in the lane that gave us our first lead of the game at 19–18, Colton Banner called timeout.

I gathered the guys together. My lungs felt as if they were on fire. Curtis's ankle looked as though his coin collection was duct-taped to it. Stretch was gassed and hurting.

"We've got them on the run," I said. "Let's finish it."

Neither of the guys had the strength to respond. I drained the last of my water bottle and took a couple of deep breaths. Win or lose, I would know I'd given it everything I had.

It was ball out to the Future Jayhawks. We could withstand a basket inside the two-point line because that would only knot it up at nineteen apiece, and we could win it on the next possession.

But if we gave up a two-pointer from beyond the arc, the Future Jayhawks could stick a fork in us because we'd be done.

It was simple: we needed a stop and a hoop to take the title.

39

Hello, Zeke, It's Been a While

It had all came down to one moment in time, the kind I'd played out in my head or on the court at the rec center a bazillion times: get a stop, make a shot, take home the trophy.

Curtis and Stretch and I took our time getting back onto the court to conserve whatever energy we had left, which wasn't much. The Future Jayhawks had barely broken a sweat up to that point. They had to know we had zero left in the tank, and they seemed to enjoy a boost of confidence because of it.

My basketball instincts told me they would try to work the ball down low for an easy bucket because they thought they could stop us on defense afterward and then take us out using the same strategy on the next possession. The arena's horn sounded. The fans hushed and rose to their feet.

The referee blew his whistle. "Officials' timeout!" he shouted as he pointed toward a pool of perspiration on the court and waved for a member of the maintenance crew to bring a mop.

A janitor stepped out onto the court. It was Dr. Naismith. The long-deceased icon who had invented basketball at a YMCA training school in Springfield, Massachusetts, in 1891 stood at the Allen Fieldhouse free-throw line mopping sweat that had dripped from players at a high school three-on-three tournament. It was the textbook definition of irony.

Dr. Naismith handled the chore, then whispered something to me as he walked off the court.

Stretch hustled over. "What'd the janitor say?" he asked.

"He told me to tell you to guard the paint like your life depended on it," I said.

Dr. Naismith hadn't really said that, but it wouldn't have surprised me if he had, because everyone in the arena knew the Future Jayhawks would work the ball in deep for the sure bucket.

Stretch persisted. "C'mon, man, what'd he say?"

What Dr. Naismith actually said was meant for my ears only. He told me I could never tell anyone about the 7th Dimension or my encounter with him, but I didn't have to evade Stretch's questioning any longer because I was saved by the referee's whistle.

"Ball out to the Future Jayhawks."

Stretch picked up Jack Diamond, who anchored himself at the corner of the free-throw line. Curtis guarded Tripp Wheeler, who stood at half-court to inbound the ball. I covered Colton

Banner, who set up on the left wing. The ref handed the ball to Tripp. With Curtis hawking him, Tripp slapped the basketball with his hand to signal the start of a play.

Then the unexpected happened.

Jack darted over to set a pick on me. Colton ran me into the screen and caught the inbounds pass wide open above the two-point arc at the top of the key. Stretch was under my instructions to protect against an easy layup, so he didn't come out to help, and I was hopelessly out of position.

Colton took a one-bounce dribble to steady himself and leaped high into the air for an uncontested jumper from distance.

Swish.

Ballgame.

The Future Jayhawks had beaten us, 20–19, to win the title. The roar of the crowd rumbled through my ears. We stood in shock as the Future Jayhawks celebrated at mid-court. Stretch bent over, hands on his hips, sucking in as much air as his lungs would allow. Curtis, balancing himself on two wobbly ankles, looked like he'd just missed catching the biggest wave of his life. I stood alone, wondering how I'd misread the Future Jayhawks' strategy on that final play.

Colton provided the explanation. "We knew we couldn't stop you," he said. "The only chance we had was to go for the deuce to end it, so you couldn't touch the ball again. I miss that shot, it's your hardware."

I'd sure blown that. I'd figured they thought they could stop us. Turned out the Future Jayhawks didn't think they could stop *me.* It was easy to see why Colton was the KU basketball program's top recruit. He was skilled, smart, and honorable. I would have enjoyed being his teammate.

Colton and I bro-hugged and said goodbye as the PA announcer made it official. "Congratulations to the Future Jayhawks, winners of this year's western regional three-on-three tournament. You can see these young fellas play right here at Allen Fieldhouse this season. And you boys from McDerney Continuation, you have a safe trip home."

Those last words brought me back to reality. I needed to get all of us home safely, especially Lawrence, but first I had to wrap my head around all that had happened over the past couple of days. I wasn't sure where to start.

"Can I have my keys?"

I turned around to find Wade in a crisp military uniform minus a pant leg, his left leg in a thick cast, arms outstretched.

His warm embrace felt like home.

"I was so worried about you," I said. "Mom, too. What happened?"

"What happened?" Wade said. "After you busted my Chevy out of cold storage, Chett Biffmann called Mom and rolled over on you, that's what."

"No, I mean what happened to your leg?"

"We took enemy fire while protecting some kids at a school in Kandahar. Would you believe they were playing basketball at the time?"

Yep, I believed it—no doubt the 7th Dimension in action dismantling the game. Add it to the list of worldwide basketball calamities I was responsible for. Some future guardian of the game I'd turned out to be.

I stood at center court feeling sorry for myself as Curtis and Stretch packed their gym bags and joined us.

"You're several inches taller than the last time I saw you," Wade said to Stretch. "Looks like your dad's been feeding you."

"Not enough, dude," Curtis said. "After he finishes dinner at his place, he comes over to mine for a second helping."

"Shaka brah," Wade said. "How are they breakin' back home?"

"Gnarly, bud," Curtis said. "Six-foot grinders at Zuma last week, off the Richter, totally primo."

Curtis, like all of us, was happy to see Wade alive and well. All was right in my world, at least in that moment, a welcome relief after recent events, which turned everything upside down. I scanned the upper rows for any sign of Lawrence but couldn't locate him. Just then, someone else found me.

"Hello, Zeke, it's been a while."

It was Coach Worth.

40

Won't Be Needing These Anymore

I was surprised that Coach Worth would take the time to stop by and say hello. After the university rescinded my basketball scholarship, I didn't think there was much left to talk about.

"Hey, Coach, good to see you again," I said. "These are my teammates, Curtis Short and Stretch Puckett, and that's my brother, Wade."

"Gentlemen, it's nice to meet you," Coach Worth said. "What happened to that leg, marine?"

"Guess you could say it was a basketball-related field injury," Wade said. "I should be back in the lineup in no time."

"Glad to hear that. Speaking of getting back in the lineup, can I have a word with you in private, Zeke?"

What could Coach Worth have to say to me that he couldn't say in front of Wade and the guys? Maybe he'd found out that I'd gained unauthorized access to the arena and wanted to reprimand me with minimal embarrassment. Perhaps he wanted to tell me that my strategy on the final play was flawed.

"Those are some jim-dandy uniforms," Coach Worth said as he chuckled. "If we handed out a trophy for the best-dressed team, you fellas would certainly be in the hunt."

"I'm just glad I had a chance to experience what it was like to play on this court."

Coach Worth's face turned serious. "I wanted to talk to you about that," he said. "I'm real sorry about the way things worked out with your scholarship. My hands were tied on that whole deal."

"No need to explain, Coach."

"I was impressed with how you handled yourself today. It wasn't easy coming into this place and representing like that. You showed me a lot of skill and poise."

Sure—and a faulty game plan in which I allowed myself to be taken out of the play when we had to lock down on defense. The coach was giving me more credit than I deserved.

"Thanks, Coach."

"How are your grades?"

I told him they were good. Even though I'd been expelled from Southland Central, I'd enrolled at McDerney right away and continued to hit the books.

"I think Admissions will recertify your transcripts, so I'm offering you a chance to walk on and try out for the team in the fall," Coach Worth said. "No scholarship in the first year. No promises, either. Just an opportunity to come to Lawrence, Kansas, and prove yourself."

I felt a surge of nervous energy shudder through my body. Coach Worth was offering me another shot at achieving the biggest goal of my life. I knew if I studied the system and trained hard, I could make the team.

Of course, I would need to get a job in Los Angeles right away and work all summer to save money. I'd also have to take out student loans and find a part-time job in Lawrence as soon as I arrived in the fall. There was much to do in a short period of time, but I knew I could handle it.

"What do you think?" Coach Worth asked.

What did he think I thought? I glanced at all the championship banners circling the arena. I saw my friends and my brother standing a few feet away straining to pick up remnants of my conversation with Coach Worth. Somehow, I'd managed a shot at redemption after nearly costing the world the sport of basketball.

Then I thought about my friends and family back home in Los Angeles, all the people who supported me unconditionally in good times and bad. If I left my support system behind in order to seek redemption, was it just another form of running away from my problems?

"I really appreciate the offer, Coach, but I'm going to have to pass." I didn't know how I managed to get those words out.

Coach Worth grimaced. "How's that?"

By then, Wade and the guys had almost turned blue from holding their collective breath, trying to pick up any shred of our conversation.

"I've got commitments back home I need to honor," I said. "We have a great community college nearby. I'm going to try out for the team there, so maybe we can pick up this conversation in a couple of years, if the door is still open."

"It will be," the coach said. "Coach Kincaid is solid. You'll do well there. Best of luck, and I *will* see you in a couple of years."

I was sure Coach Worth hadn't expected me to turn down his offer, but he seemed to understand my reasons, and he knew enough about the basketball program at Jefferson Community College to endorse Coach Kincaid. He said goodbye and headed for the exit as Curtis and Stretch accosted me for information.

"What'd he say?" Stretch asked.

"Yeah, what went down?" Curtis said.

"He told me I should dump you losers and get some real teammates. I told him I had no argument."

Curtis and Stretch knew me well enough to understand I wouldn't reveal the nature of my conversation with Coach Worth. Wade didn't ask, because he'd already figured it out.

There was one more reason I turned down the coach's offer. That reason walked onto the court and handed me a folded-up piece of paper.

"I've been looking all over for you," I said to Lawrence. "Where've you been?"

Lawrence pointed to the note. I unfolded it and read it to myself:

Good news, bad news. The good news is, the 7th Dimension was swayed by your selfless attempt to save the game, so it reversed its decision. First time it's ever done that. The bad news is, it suspended your basketball guardianship appointment indefinitely. Last thing: I thought Dr. Naismith was a stand-up guy.

Lawrence was a man of few words. They were usually right on the button. I folded the note back up and slid it into my duffel bag as I waved my brother over. "Wade, this is my friend Lawrence. Lawrence, Wade."

"Pleased to meet you," Wade said. "Any friend of Zeke's is a friend of mine."

Lawrence didn't say anything. No surprise there. But then he amazed all of us by extending his hand to Wade.

"Where's the Chevy?" Wade asked as they shook hands.

Lawrence gave him the keys, picked up his metal case, and headed for the exit.

"C'mon," I said. "Follow him."

"Why did the kid have my car keys?" Wade said as he gave them to me, knowing full well he wouldn't be able to negotiate the clutch with his left leg in a cast.

"Don't ask."

We grabbed our gear and followed Lawrence to the parking lot where he'd stashed Wade's truck. Wade and I had plenty of time to get Lawrence and the guys to the Greyhound terminal for the bus that would depart at 5:50 p.m. for Los

Angeles. As everyone piled in, Lawrence handed me another note:

Lawrence Memorial Cemetery Park,
1517 East 15th Street, 2.6 miles east.

"We're making a stop on the way," I announced to everyone as I turned the engine over and threw the truck into first gear.

I parked in front of the entrance to the cemetery a few minutes later. Lawrence got out of the truck and walked along the grass toward a granite memorial in the center of the park. I cut the engine and followed him.

Lawrence knelt down at the base of the memorial, removed the seven pencils from his pocket protector, and interconnected them for the last time in the heptagonal figure I had come to know so well.

"Won't be needing these anymore," he said as he walked past me and back toward the truck.

I studied the brass plaque mounted on the front of the memorial, the final resting place of Dr. James Naismith. I read the tribute silently to myself:

Born November 6, 1861 in Almonte, Ontario, Canada and died November 28, 1939 in Lawrence, Kansas. Buried in Lawrence Memorial Park.

Dr. Naismith invented the game of basketball as a winter indoor sport for the YMCA at Springfield, Massachusetts in 1891.

In 1898 he accepted a position at the University of Kansas. His goal was to develop the University's Physical Education Department. He also agreed to accept the coaching position of K.U.'s first basketball team.

K.U.'s first games were played either in a local low ceiling roller skating rink or away from home due to the poor facilities at K.U. Naismith was instrumental in the development of the first modern gymnasium for basketball, the old "Robinson Gym" on the K.U. campus.

The Naismith Basketball Hall of Fame in Springfield, Massachusetts is named after him. He was elected posthumously to the Naismith Basketball Hall of Fame in 1959.

He also was a 32nd Degree Mason.

Directly below the inscription was the University of Kansas mascot, a Jayhawk, just like the cartoon bird at center court in Allen Fieldhouse—and just like the mysterious bird Lawrence had seen on the highway just outside Grand Junction. It was the final piece to a basketball puzzle that stretched all the way from the rec center in Los Angeles to eastern Kansas.

We drove to the bus terminal. Wade waited in the Chevy as I bought Lawrence's ticket and walked him and the guys to the waiting Greyhound.

"Want a piece of gum?"

"Nah, I'm good," I said. "When you get home, tell your dad I'm sorry for keeping you out for so long."

Wade and I waved goodbye as the bus pulled away. We drove back to Los Angeles, stopping in Denver along the way to visit our father. Wade and Dad worked on the truck while I worked on my jump shot in the driveway, just like old times.

On the final leg of the journey home, Wade told me it was Vice Principal Littwack who had arranged for his transportation from the military hospital in Germany to Kansas City International Airport. Mr. Littwack had learned about Wade being wounded in action and my invitation to the western regional tournament from none other than Mr. Brock Decker.

Mr. Littwack and Brock Decker, working in harmony on my behalf.

Hadn't seen *that* coming.

41

Thanks for Being My Friend

Wade and I drove halfway across the country and made it back to our apartment on Wednesday night, four days after the tournament. Mom was waiting for us with dinner in the oven and tears in her eyes. We were together again, at least for a short period of time, three quarters of an original family of four.

After my first good night's sleep in a long time, I was back at McDerney the next morning pushing open the double doors to the cafeteria. It was a gentle shove, the kind that makes the doors fall short of their protective doorstops before drifting back to their original closed position. I guess you could say I was paying closer attention to my actions and learning from my mistakes. Mom's handwritten note explaining my three-day absence from school was enough to keep me out of detention.

"Zeke, over here!"

It was Stretch, standing and waving me over to our table. Was it just me, or did the Tall One look even taller than the last time I'd seen him five days earlier? As I made my way over, I saw Lawrence at his table in back, pouring hot water from a thermos into a bowl of freeze-dried chili mac 'n' beef. When he noticed me, he waved. There's a first time for everything.

I studied Stretch more closely. "Why do you look geekier to me?" I said.

"I grew another inch on the bus ride home. I'm seven feet even."

"Dude, how's the air up there?" Curtis said.

"Heavy pizza, strong chance of body spray."

I set my basketball down on the fourth chair that we used as a blocker to ward off outsiders.

"How was that long drive, bro?" Curtis said.

"Long," I said as we began our ritual of discovering what the others had brought for lunch. "American cheese on egg bread, squared-off carrot spears on the side."

"You ever ask your mom why she cuts your carrots like that?" Stretch said.

"It's a mom thing. She likes to remind me that I'm as unique as a square carrot in a world of round ones."

"Unique, or more dweeb-like?"

It was Brock Decker. I no longer knew what to make of him. Our relationship seemed to get more complicated as time went on. All at once, we were former friends, archrivals, and possible future teammates. Throw into the mix the recent-development wildcard—Brock was the stepbrother of the girl I liked who wanted nothing more to do with me. "Let me guess: you missed the last three days of school to work on your defense," Brock said.

"Stand down, private." Vice Principal Littwack never minced words. "Don't you have somewhere to be other than standing in the way of Ezekiel enjoying time with his friends?"

"See ya, dweeb," Brock said as he retreated to the cafeteria's cement-head table.

"How's Wade?" Mr. Littwack said.

"He's good. Mom's home-cooked meals will help."

I was grateful to Mr. Littwack for running interference on Wade's behalf and fast-tracking his transportation back to the states. Wade had never told me that he shared a connection with Mr. Littwack.

"Was just curious, sir, how you knew my brother?"

"I've never met him."

"Sir?"

"I guess I owe you an explanation," Mr. Littwack said. "We Littwacks are fifth-generation marines. Wade and my grandson Cannon met quite by chance in Afghanistan a year ago when Cannon was on a reconnaissance mission in a small village on the outskirts of Kabul."

Mr. Littwack explained that when Cannon's communications unit came under attack, members of the Marine Corps Forces Special Operations Command were called in to restore order. Wade was part of that group.

"Cannon was wounded, losing a lot of blood. Your brother threw Cannon over his shoulder and carried him out of there in the middle of a fierce gun battle."

Mr. Littwack told me that Wade had helped stop the bleeding until a chopper came to take Cannon and other wounded marines to a medical unit.

"Saved his life," Mr. Littwack said, his voice cracking. "When I heard Wade was laid up at the regional medical center in Germany, I started working the phones."

"I appreciate what you did for my brother, sir."

"Stick with basketball, Ezekiel. You'll live longer."

It was advice I planned to take, but first there was a cheese sandwich with my name on it. As I unwrapped it, Stretch pulled a thermos from his lunchbox and unscrewed the lid. I thought I was seeing things when he tore off the top of a foil-wrapped brick of lasagna with meat sauce, dumped it into a bowl, and poured hot water over it.

"What in the world?"

"What? It's just lunch," Stretch said.

Then Curtis, a vegetarian, unzipped a package of freeze-dried pasta primavera.

I looked up from our table to see everyone else in the cafeteria preparing lunch from a foil pouch: beef stroganoff with noodles, chicken and dumplings, seafood chowder, sweet-and-sour pork, and turkey Tetrazzini, as far as the eye could see.

"Stuff's not bad," Stretch said. "Could use a little salt, though."

"I don't think I got the memo," I said.

"There wasn't one," said a familiar voice behind me.

I turned around. It was Rebecca.

"If you'd been around for, like, the last few days, you

would've known I declared today to be Lawrence Appreciation Day." It was wonderful to see Rebecca again, even though I had no idea what she was talking about. "You should check in with Lawrence."

I tried to find the right words to apologize to Rebecca for making a fool of myself when I went to her house and found Brock Decker there before I left for Kansas.

"You know, that thing at your place with Brock, I wanted to say—"

"To say what a jerk you were?"

"I didn't realize it was your nose that I broke, and when I saw Brock, I kinda lost it. I'm really sorry."

"Tell you what," Rebecca said. "You can make up for it by walking me home from school." Then Rebecca did the unexpected. She leaned in and kissed me—smack dab on the lips.

"Sure thing. See you after sixth period."

I floated on air over to Lawrence's table to find out what he had done that was important enough to warrant having a day named after him. "How pissed was your dad when you got home?"

Lawrence didn't answer, but he handed me an envelope. I opened it and read the letter inside:

Dear Sherman:

We are pleased to inform you that you have been accepted into the California Institute of Technology summer internship program as an apprentice spaceflight mathematician in the Division of Physics, Mathematics, and Astronomy.

"Congratulations, pal of mine. Looks like you're on the fast track to the Red Planet."

Lawrence stood up from his chair. I extended my hand to him. As he shook it, I looked into his eyes and noticed they were looking back at mine—for the first time since I'd met him. Lawrence was strong and confident, his green eyes clear and bright.

"Thanks for being my friend," he said.

"Back atcha, buddy."

I knew that kids with autism sometimes have trouble looking people in the eye because there is so much going on in their minds that they find direct visual input too distracting. It was heartwarming that Lawrence was comfortable enough around me for all the tumblers in his mind to fall into place.

Brock, Rebecca, Curtis, Stretch, and I graduated from McDerney a few weeks after Lawrence Appreciation Day.

Lawrence aced his summer internship at Caltech and returned to McDerney as a quirky but confident senior. Wade's leg healed and he rejoined his unit in Afghanistan. I was sad to see him go, but being a marine was his calling.

The guys and I spent most of our idle time that summer at the rec center working on our game. Brock stopped by once in a while to join us as the glacier that had stood between us for so many years began to melt. Rebecca applied to universities around the state that had well-regarded sports medicine programs.

We enrolled at Jefferson Community College in the fall. Curtis signed up for philosophy classes. Stretch went in as a criminal justice major. I took up journalism. Brock, always the undecided one, listed his major as undeclared.

Rebecca was accepted into three different universities but decided at the eleventh hour to join us at Jefferson.

Basketball team tryouts were set for the first Friday morning of the new semester at 9:00 a.m. The guys and I looked forward to playing for Coach Kincaid, but first we had to make the team.

42

Stranger Things Have Happened

"Ezekiel, wake up. Don't you have basketball tryouts this morning?" That was my mom. Good grief, I'd overslept.

"What time is it?"

"It's eight thirty, son. I've got your breakfast on the table."

I was sunk. Was it possible to be cut from a basketball team you'd never gone out for?

Tryouts were at 9:00 a.m. sharp, and Coach Kincaid didn't mess around. I'd already missed one deadline with him. I couldn't afford for that to happen a second time or I'd spend the basketball season refereeing youth games at the park. I threw on my gym clothes and grabbed my ball.

"Your breakfast!"

"Sorry, Mom, no time!" I hustled my bike out the front door and down the apartment stairs.

"Cheese 'n' crackers, Zeke. What's all the racket?"

"Not now, Mrs. Fenner!"

It was 8:35. The bike ride to Jefferson, under the best conditions, took thirty minutes. I flew down Chamberlain Drive, dodging cars and pedestrians all the way to the college, then weaved across campus to the gym, propped my bike against the foyer wall, and threw open the double doors.

The noise from the crash bar startled Coach Kincaid, who stood in front of two dozen student athletes hoping to make the team. I looked up at the clock: 9:05. I saw Curtis and Stretch standing together, worried looks on their faces. Brock was there too, but he was grinning.

"Nice of you to join us, Zeke," Coach Kincaid said.

"It's good to be here, Coach." Geez, did I really just say that?

"You know basketball tryouts started promptly at nine, right?"

"Yes, sir."

"You know you're five minutes late *again*?"

"Yes, sir."

Coach Kincaid removed his cap and scratched his head as if pondering a weighty decision. "What am I supposed to do about this?"

I answered without thinking it all the way through. "Do you think you could make an exception?" I tried to stop my mouth from forming the words, but it was too late. The horse was already out of the barn.

Coach Kincaid didn't hesitate with his response: "An exception? Sure, Zeke. Instead of the entire team running twenty laps around the gym because you're late, everyone will do forty."

The players erupted in a group groan. On the seventh lap, Brock accelerated and passed me so he could weigh in. "Thanks a lot, dweeb."

I made the team and earned the starting point guard position. Curtis was a reserve shooting guard, coming off the bench whenever we needed a sure bucket late. Stretch, standing at seven feet, two inches by the time the regular season opened, was Coach Kincaid's automatic choice for center. Brock made the team, playing mostly as an on-you-like-glue guard when we needed to shut down an opposing player who had a hot shooting hand.

Right now I'm sitting on my bed at home resting for tonight's game, the Southern California regional championship. The game will be at Jefferson, the site of my previous attempt at a school title. That one didn't go so well. I'm optimistic my team will have a different result tonight.

Curtis was voted winner of the MVT award for the team's Most Valuable Tan at last night's team dinner. His semester so far has consisted of surfing, basketball, schoolwork, and surfing.

Stretch still helps his dad with painting chores, but his sights are set on a career as a private eye. His chances of success will improve if he can stop growing.

Lawrence's internship at Caltech led to another internship,

this time at the Jet Propulsion Laboratory in Pasadena. Despite a busy academic schedule, the whiz kid attended all of our home games, sitting high in the stands and using advanced algorithms to calculate my shooting percentages and efficiency on the fast break.

Rebecca has a class in the college's Kinesiology Department as a sports medicine trainee, so she attends the basketball games and looks after Brock and me and the other guys. Rebecca and I started going steady a couple of weeks into the semester and have been inseparable ever since. She still gets on my case all the time, but it feels different, because I know she cares about me.

Life with Brock Decker as my teammate again is challenging but less awkward than before. We're mending our friendship, one basketball game at a time.

Wade sends the occasional letter from Afghanistan and manages to stay out of harm's way. He's supposed to be coming home for good in the spring.

My dad writes to me more often than he used to. I'm hoping to travel to Denver during summer break to spend time with him.

Chip's Sporting Goods has enjoyed record sales in the basketball equipment section ever since Chip repaired the meteorite damage. Shortly after the grand reopening, Global Mega-Sports offered to purchase the store in a deal that would have included a name change to Chip's Global Mega-Sports and Chip staying on as general manager for a couple of years, but he politely turned down the offer because he didn't think it was in the best interests of his customers.

As for the status of my basketball guardianship appointment, I don't have any news to report. Lawrence says the 7th Dimension altered its spectral broadcast subcarrier again and he hasn't been able to tap into the correct non-neutral linear half-frequency, so it's all quiet on the Entity front.

Odds are I won't get another chance at that guardianship, but stranger things have happened in my life. Much stranger.

Acknowledgments

A lifetime of road traveling went into the creation of this debut novel. I'm grateful to the people in my life who contributed in the form of love, friendship, and editorial insight.

The list starts with my editor, Judy Gitenstein, who guided me through the editorial process with skill, grace, and compassion. What a blessing it was to have found her.

Christopher Caines served as my intrepid copyeditor. His level of expertise with the written word was only exceeded by his sense of humor and knowledge of basketball.

My book producer Marco Pavia, a man who is equal parts psychologist, camp counselor, and shaman, handled the design, marketing, production, and distribution chores.

Tabitha Lahr applied her creative vision as cover designer, interpreting the story's essence in starkly elegant images.

Brent Wilcox lent his talents as the book's unflappable interior page designer, combining a keen sense of style with saintly patience.

My fastidious proofreaders were Sara Dyck and Cecile Garcia, each going far beyond the call of duty as they meticulously unearthed ill-chosen words.

Kaitlin Menear offered sage advice and a much-needed reality check in the early stages of the outline.

Samuel Adam "Shmuli" Weber served as inspiration for Lawrence, the book's driving force.

Sam Hertzog agreed to accept the position of flagship teenage beta reader. I wish I had a buck ninety-eight for every time he pulled me up short on the first draft. Sam's parents, Steven and Ann Hertzog, generously offered logistical support and a spare bedroom at their residential command post in Lawrence, Kansas.

My Los Angeles-based beta readers were Paul Duff, Joe Kuzma, Jill Moreno, Jamie Kuzma, Bobbie Yunis, Sidney Montgomery, Ruby Vickers, Hailey Star Dowthwaite, Carson Tujague, and Claira Brown.

Abbi Huderle, director of the Booth Family Hall of Athletics at the University of Kansas, shared her deep knowledge of the origins of basketball during our tour of the athletic museum at Allen Fieldhouse.

Andrea Hudy, KU's assistant athletic director for sports performance, graciously offered a behind-the-scenes look at the athletic facilities, which included a discussion of what might or might not be happening in the chilly rafters of Allen Fieldhouse in the dead of night when no one was around to bear witness.

Many of the historical facts pertaining to Dr. James Naismith and the invention of "Basket Ball" were drawn from the book *James Naismith: The Man Who Invented Basketball* by Rob

Rains with Hellen Carpenter (Philadelphia: Temple University Press, 2009). It's a wonderful resource that I recommend to anyone interested in learning more about a remarkable educator, medical doctor, and minister.

I'd also like to acknowledge the syndicated radio program *Coast to Coast AM* with George Noory for helping to expand my horizons and explore alternate ways of looking at our world and beyond.

Bob Conroy, engineering faculty member emeritus from Cal Poly San Luis Obispo, lent a skilled hand with the mathematical and scientific aspects of the book.

Denfield Gomes served as my trusted military advisor.

Los Angeles Valley College journalism professor Henry A. Lalane spent an entire semester diagramming sentences on the blackboard in a course called Mechanics of Expression. His classroom was the place where my journey as a writer began.

My high school basketball coach, Burt Golden, helped shape my life in so many ways, most notably by instilling the concept of seeing the ball go through the hoop in your mind's eye before you shoot it, a philosophy that has extended to other parts of my world through the years.

My twelve teammates on the varsity basketball team at Van Nuys High School are living proof of the power of teamwork. They are Lloyd Waxman, Gregg Chisolm, Bob Wells, Marty Lieberman, Larry Freedman, Jim Segafredo, Gavin Smith, Ron Emord, Jim Clermont, Rick Garcia, Doug Andersen, and Tony Petru.

My friend and former boss Jim Gentilcore lived up to his

name as he encouraged me to embrace my gifts by using them for the good of others.

I attended a memorial service for Beryl Brady, mother of a close friend, at the chapel of ease within the walls of Mission San Fernando Rey de España, the seventeenth of the California Missions. I received the ethereal gift of my story concept during that solemn event. I haven't been back to the mission since, but I plan to return when I embark on the outline for my second novel.

The Roman Catholic monks of the New Camaldoli Hermitage in Big Sur continue to provide inspiration, divine or otherwise.

I have a small group of sportswriter and journalist friends whose expertise and influence can be found in these pages. They are Cary Osborne, Bob Dickson, Mason Nesbitt, Paul McLeod, Vimal Patel, Brandon Lowrey, Dan Agnew, Joey Gulino, Grant Parpan, Erik Boal, Perry Smith, Don McLean, and Scott "Ned" Galetti.

The coaches and administrators at College of the Canyons were generous with their time and insight. Their commitment to student athletes and student journalists is inspiring. They are Chuck Lyon, Philip Marcellin, Garett Tujague, Len Mohney, Celina Baguiao, Jesse Muñoz, Greg Herrick, Howard Fisher, Lee Smelser, Chris Cota, Lindie Kane, Ted Iacenda, Lisa Hooper, Gary Peterson, Nick Carter, Mike Halcovich, Ray Whitten, Diana Stanich, and Jim Ruebsamen.

A lifetime of choosing friends and coworkers wisely has produced many trusted allies and spirit guides who helped shape my writing life. I'd like to acknowledge my debt of gratitude to

Ted Dayton, Neal Laybhen, Rob Anker, Steve "Junior" Aronson, Mark Baarstad, Mike Harris, Craig Anderson, Susan and Monte Dunham, Cheyenne Nicole Dunham, Fran Graziano, Randie and Ron Hauss, Leo Bunnin, John Walker, Steve Williams, Angela Weber, Herb Brady, Jane Hawley, Pat Collins, Richard Andrews, Jasmine Ilkhan, Theresa Wescott, Julieanne Reall, Dean Beattie, Steve Ladley, Bill Sullivan, Tad Marburg, Chris Coppel, Kurt Schwenk, Brian Minkoff, Jeff Miller, Theo Gluck, Clark Peterson, Mickie Zupancic, Michael Kadenacy, Dawn Walock, Darryl Mardirossian, Kurt Kusenko, Sarah Ellis, Marty Lamadrid, Steve Waugh, Kip Sears, Chris Witham, Gregg Sandheinrich, Gary Bric, Bob Perkins, John Blum, Julie Peña, Greg Brown, Steve "Big Stix" Cantos, John Burnley, Steven G. Smith, Susan Roberts, Candy Johnson, Bernie Larsen, Todd and Mary Goodson, Andrea Giambrone, Priscilla Pesci, Jason Dravis and Travis Stewart, Michael Benner, Max and Audrey Johnson, Jeff and Jana Hammond, Carol Perata, Jerry Simpson, Corbin Meyer, Mike Hulyk, Erik Peterson, Alvin Lee, Reno Wilde, and the real Chett Biffmann, wherever he is.

Family is the foundation of my life. My parents, Jack and Anne Leener, gave me breath and provided a safe and nurturing home. My dad imparted his writing gene, while my mom made sure I always made it to basketball practice on time.

My big sister, Kathy, was pretty cool and seldom bratty, and her husband, Andy Gordon, remains a trusted ally. I've never said thanks to my younger brother, Doug, for rebounding for me in the backyard as I was perfecting my mid-range jumper, so this will serve that purpose. His wife, Jennifer, has always been a positive force.

My nephews, Jared Leener and Brian Bunnin, help keep me young, as do Brian's wife, Cathy, and their sons, Max and Bennett.

My good friends Stephen and Suzy Bookbinder introduced me to my wife, so they get special recognition here, as do my wife's parents, Ken and Annette Fein, who gave me the benefit of the doubt when I was writing this novel instead of looking for an actual job.

My son, Zachary Leener, has long been the sounding board and human litmus test for every creative endeavor I've undertaken. Zak and his wife, Erika, inspire me in ways that words cannot adequately describe.

Finally, I want to acknowledge the beautiful spirit and utter awesomeness of my wife, Andrea, who makes everything in my life possible.

About the Author

Craig Leener got his start in organized basketball at the age of nine in a Southern California YMCA youth league on a team called the Monsters. He later secured a roster spot on the varsity squad at Van Nuys High School, where he was considered to be the thirteenth-best basketball player on a team of thirteen players.

Craig earned an associate degree in liberal arts from Los Angeles Valley College and a bachelor's degree in radio, TV, and film from California State University, Northridge. While at CSUN, he served as a board operator at campus radio station KCSN 88.5 FM, engineering live broadcasts of men's basketball games. Today he sits on the board of directors of CSUN's Journalism Alumni Association, where he mentors student journalists.

Craig worked in human resources management within the entertainment industry for many years before landing his dream job as a sports journalist at *The Signal* newspaper in Santa Clarita, California. One summer, while working as a staff writer for *The Signal*, he traveled to every Major League Baseball stadium with his son, Zachary, delivering a series of articles from the road on fathers and sons and baseball.

Craig is a member of the North Valley Family YMCA in northern Los Angeles County and lives in the suburbs of Los Angeles with his wife, Andrea, and their two mischievous but well-meaning dogs, Sophie and Beau. He purports to be an eighty-seven-percent free-throw shooter on his backyard home court, a claim that has never been independently verified.

He is a passionate, lifelong opponent of the instant replay in sports.

This Was Never About Basketball is Craig's debut novel.

Turn the page for a preview!

1

Magical Things Could Happen

I had practiced *the play* on the rec center's basketball court a million times before.

Now, on a spring afternoon in Los Angeles, I was running it for real, in the biggest game of my life—the Southern California Regional Championship—on our home court, the gymnasium at Jefferson Community College.

My name is Zeke Archer, and that's where this strange tale begins.

My stories always begin with basketball. And it's through basketball that I measure my life and figure out the people who are in it. I am more confident on a basketball court than I am anywhere else on earth.

The game, which was taught to me years ago by my older brother, Wade, always reveals the truth.

Our team was on defense and trailing our crosstown rivals from Westside City College, 77–76, with ten seconds left to go, when the Westside coach called a timeout to draw up his team's final play. It was a good thing he did too—we were out of timeouts and running on fumes.

The crowd stirred and buzzed as our coach, Coach Kincaid, waved us over to the sideline. Our shooting guard, Curtis Short, playing on a sprained ankle, plopped down onto the bench, his face contorted in pain. Our seven-foot-two-inch center, Roland "Stretch" Puckett, cranked his lanky frame forward, hands on hips, gasping for oxygen.

Curtis and Stretch were my best friends. Curtis's devotion to basketball was exceeded only by his love of surfing. Stretch's desire for a career as a private investigator was eclipsed only by his fondness for food.

Our two forwards, Brock Decker and Jed Swagerty, weren't in much better shape. They were winded and drenched in sweat.

Coach Kincaid had a knack for calming us down when the pressure was mounting and the stakes were high. He set down his clipboard and glanced at the scoreboard.

"It's only one point, gentlemen, and ten seconds is an eternity," Coach Kincaid said. "Man-to-man defense. Go for the steal on the inbounds pass. If you don't get it, foul whoever catches the ball. We'll put him on the free-throw line and win it on the other end."

Sure thing, Coach. Simple enough. Do the near impossible in less time than it takes to lace up a pair of high-tops—and do it on an empty tank.

"Got it, Coach," I said. "C'mon, guys, let's go get us some hardware."

That's what my teammates expected me to say, because I was Jefferson's team captain and all-conference point guard. But beyond the mere words, I really believed we could pull it off. The hardware up for grabs was the So-Cal championship trophy.

The referee blew his whistle and handed the basketball to the Westside player who was taking it out of bounds. The kid slapped the ball with his hand, cuing his teammates to dart around the court in all directions in search of daylight. I turned my back on the guy I was guarding to make it seem as if I were going after a different player. Then I waited a beat, whirled around, and stepped into my opponent's path.

I intercepted the inbounds pass, setting into motion *the play*—a three-on-two fast break. Wade had once told me that if I ran a fast break to perfection, magical things could happen.

Wade was in the Marine Corps, in Afghanistan, serving our country in a war on the other side of the globe. I would have settled for the magical thing being Wade shouting encouragement and instructions from the bleachers. But he was a few weeks away from coming home to Los Angeles for good, so that wasn't an option. Instead, I would have to figure out how to win it without him.

The fast break is an offensive strategy in which the point guard takes the ball up court so swiftly that the defense doesn't have a chance to set up. My job in that moment was to maneuver the ball across half court and force the two outnumbered, back-pedaling defenders to commit to a defensive plan of action. Once they did, I would choose my best option—pass to an open teammate for a layup, take the shot from the free-throw line, or dish off to a teammate trailing the play behind me for a mid-range jumper.

And I needed to decide by the time I got to the charity stripe fifteen feet from the basket. I had to make a split-second decision and live with the consequences.

I took off down court as Curtis speed-shuffled across the hardwood to my right. Stretch filled the lane on my left, galloping like a giraffe pursued by a starving lion. Fans rose to their feet as the two Westside defenders scrambled backward. *The play* we had practiced so many times before was unfolding right before my eyes.

Perfectly.

Then, when I pulled up at the free-throw line, it happened. My life, as they say, would never be the same.